DINER

of

LOST SOULS

a mystery thriller

Graham DIAMOND   Hedy CAMPEAS

Print ISBN 978-1-66783-330-9
eBook ISBN 978-1-66783-331-6

Lion Press, New York

Dedicated to the wonderful people of Greece

Wherever they may live.

DINER

of

LOST
SOULS

1

AFTER WHISTLING LOUDLY BETWEEN HIS teeth, the first driver yelled, "Move your damned truck!"

The disturbance outside woke her. Cora raised herself on one elbow and peered from the window. Two trucks, one a big dry van and the other a refrigerated trailer, stood motionless. Their drivers began arguing with enthusiastic vulgarities.

Cora ignored the commotion and checked the time. Her phone read 6:17 AM. Unfocused eyes momentarily stared at the ceiling. Nagging dream memories faded. She sat up at the side of her messy bed, rubbed both hands on her strained neck, rolled her shoulders, and shook herself awake. Her back was throbbing. Helping unload crates and boxes yesterday was a bigger effort than she anticipated. Or maybe she was in denial about heavy labor at her age? If top chef Claude had shown up on time, he could have managed the entire delivery confusion himself. Claude, though, was a single father, working as hard as he could since his messy divorce. Cora empathized with his difficulty and appreciated his honesty. The early vegetable delivery arrived late, and she needed to pitch in to get everything finished in time to feed her eager, hungry customers.

In addition, her day manager Ivan was slacking off due to whatever hustle he was operating on the side. She didn't care about his private life, but it was beginning to interfere with business. That she could never allow. Finding a suitable replacement was the only solution. So, she sacked Ivan.

Tossed on his ass with two weeks' pay. She was grateful for Eddie Coltrane, already proving himself a suitable replacement. Cora Drakos ran a tight ship at the Athena Diner.

The profanities in the street continued. She pulled aside her curtain and looked. A small group of early risers and dog walkers formed a wide circle to watch the ongoing ruckus. Drivers trapped in the narrow road honked horns.

At length, the truckers told each other to fuck off, and sluggishly made their way back to their vehicles. Toxic fumes flowed from tailpipes as truck engines rumbled. The sidewalk superintendents drifted away. The nearby El train, rushing on its way to Manhattan screeched to a halt at the crowded station. The early morning circus was over.

Cora turned away, stood up, flexed muscles, and peeked at the mirror before going to the bathroom. She didn't like what she saw. Lines were beginning to etch deeper along the sides of her thin mouth. Her expressive dark eyes were becoming puffy. Due to a lack of sleep? Far too many working hours? God knows how difficult it was for her to keep up with this chaotic life.

The vivid watercolor of Athens hanging on the opposite wall greeted her like an old friend. "Hellas," she muttered, using the common name for Greece. How long was it since she'd been home? So many years. Her former life was all but buried. Could she even go back to visit after everything that happened? She blocked the thought. It was pointless to consider.

Her cell phone rang. "Yes," she murmured, stifling a yawn.

"Cora, the vegetables, they're no good--again."

"Slow down, Eddie. What's going on this time?"

"I could pick better stuff myself at any supermarket. Boss, we're paying good money for *crap.*" His voice was starting to rise. Cora stretched again as she listened and sighed. "Is everything rotten, or can we salvage some just for today? Any leftovers in the fridge? How rotten, Eddie? Take a second look while I wait. We need to be ready for breakfast traffic."

There was a momentary hesitation on the other end. "I can do whatever you need me to, Cora. I'll slice off parts of lettuce heads, chives, carrots. Maybe I can rescue the tomatoes. Radishes look okay. Most of the yellow onions are nasty. I already informed Claude."

"Good. Do what you can. I'll be there in half an hour."

"Your strong Greek coffee will be waiting."

Thank goodness for Eddie. At least she could count on him.

If Mama Annella could see me now. She looked up toward the ceiling as if it were heaven, and sadly shook her head. "Twenty years in America, Mama. More than twenty years." She raised her palms dramatically, remembering how things were after the tragedy. She quickly rejected those thoughts, swiftly picking out her clothes for the day. The diner, her diner, was ready to open its doors. Customers would be in a hurry. They always were.

"Each menu must be special," Karas Padnos, always called by his given English name, Gus, had carefully explained twenty years ago in his broken English. "Here at the Athena, we cater to neighborhood folks and also the general public." The pride in his voice was obvious. Cora casually inspected the premises with him. The diner was long and narrow, red vinyl counter seating on the right, and a line of booths on the left. Extra tables and chairs were set up around the far side.

"Especially here in what America calls ethnic neighborhoods," Gus continued, "there must be specialty foods together with staples, you understand? We cook good, hearty Greek dishes. For everyone, not just special guests." She looked up at his joyful eyes and nodded with agreement. "Our food is served by local workers. It's good because they often know and value our customers. We want everybody who comes inside to feel appreciated. Small spenders and big spenders. This ain't what's called a 'greasy spoon' in America. Everybody matters. We have truck deliveries early every day, and we buy local food when we can. You see I work hard, Cora. Extremely hard. Both with my hands and my brain. But do you know what? It's worth it. Do you understand what I'm telling you? Because at the end, it's all about the food. Our kitchen is our heart and soul. Here 'on the line' as they say. The cook is the boss in the kitchen. They watch and control order tickets while the cooking is done. Who gets served first? Who's next? Plate by plate, meal by meal. I keep my eye on quality, see? In my place that's all that ever counts—the food."

Cora understood why having ties to the community and its needs played such a vital role in achieving a restaurant's success. The Athena Diner was living proof because of Gus. It was his life.

Gus pointed here and there as they strode the premises. "We dim the lights at night," he continued with self-approval. "They start bright, but by the end of the night they turn soft. In winter dark comes early, so we keep them bright. In summer, lights don't turn on till late. Matching the light outside, understand?"

"Yes, Gus. I do understand."

"Our customers love it. It helps make them feel at home. It's good to feel at home. Tidy and neat. No dust on the windowsills."

He gestured sweepingly. "I started with nothing, but I had these two hands. And I knew what people like to eat." His chest swelled as he showed his large hands to her.

"You did good, Gus. I see what you achieved, and I admire it. All of it."

At this point he took Cora by her hand and grew somber.

"One more important thing you need to know before you come to work here. The whole place gotta be clean, see? Tables, floors, kitchen, everything. Always clean, never forget it, Cora. A dirty restaurant is no good to anybody. It sends customers running. And that I won't allow—ever."

"I understand all your instructions, Gus. Thank you for this opportunity."

He glowed with pleasure at his achievements. And now especially having this young Greek woman who had come so unexpectedly into his world. It added a pinch of spice to his delight at showing off.

"Don't worry, Cora. I'm going to teach you all of this business. Step by step. From the first egg cracked at dawn to when they pick up the trash. Soon you'll know everything that needs to be done." He threw his head back and laughed loudly as her eyes widened. "You're a smart one. I can tell. One day you'll manage the whole damn place for me."

Gus Padnos might not be formally well-educated, Cora thought, but he proved to be a clever, successful businessman. Astute and shrewd.

He remained robust for his age, muscular and strong, having trained as a wrestler and boxer during his youth in Greece. He came to America in his mid-twenties. Now in late middle age he was beefy but vigorous, his muscles firm. Human and fallible, his tanned skin was beginning to sag. His nose was prominent; his eyebrows white and thick above narrow dark eyes that judged quickly and keenly. The short-sleeved shirt owner of the Athena Diner was known as a fair but exacting employer. He paid a decent wage to loyal employees, especially the line cooks, supervisors of devoted areas in the kitchen. They were difficult to replace, and every restaurant counted on them.

Cora had stood quietly in his shadow as he barked proper detergent instructions at his sunrise shift dishwasher. Every plate, every fork, knife, and spoon must shine in the Athena Diner. From morning till night. Now, it was Cora who saw to it that it stayed that way after his passing.

Early morning sunlight streamed through the large glass windows. The smell of steaming coffee was enticing. And all these years later, Cora made certain that Gus's rules were intact. The Athena Diner remained one of the most popular in Queens. Known for fast service, healthy food in a fresh atmosphere, its name was recognized far beyond its neighborhood location. Cora had kept her promise to Gus, and the staff became her new family.

The loud rumble of the elevated subway accompanied Cora Drakos as she entered from the front door. Several of the server staff looked up, pleased to see her. She smiled her winning smile and hurried into the kitchen. The air was humid, dishes being washed in deep stainless-steel sinks. Large commercial grade freezers stood at the far end. Top of the line equipment jammed perfectly into a small space. The air was pungent with the smell of frying onions and sausage. Looking around, Cora felt the kitchen was alive with orchestrated chaos. And she loved it.

The hectic, fast paced diner atmosphere was just beginning for the breakfast take away rush. Eddie Coltrane looked up. Vegetables were piled along one side opposite the deep sinks. "This is what I was telling you, Mrs. Gus," he began, waving his hand across the assorted stacks. Cora scanned the items. He was right. Too many were spoiled. "I'll have another talk with Bruno's delivery people, Eddie. He won't want to lose us as customers. Just get today started, okay?" She walked down the crowded aisle. Early shift dishwasher Dmitri waved at her; young chef Carlos winked as he stood over a heap of scrambling eggs, home fries, and crisping bacon. The kitchen was already hot. Soon it would be sweltering.

"You've helped me work this place for how many years, Eddie? Now you're in charge."

Grinning, he replied, "Too many." This exchange had become a ritual between the hard-nosed owner and the reliable new senior manager. Eddie proved he could run the place whenever needed. Which sometimes meant from dawn till midnight.

Cora went over to the cash register to look for yesterday's receipts. "I've got them wrapped in an envelope for you," said Sara Sweeny, a sweet new-lywed who had been with Cora for less than a year, as she wiped away the residue of hand sanitizer. Bottles of the gel were strategically placed throughout. A basket of masks also stood available beside the cash register, handy for customers still wary of Covid-19 variants.

"And I've also finished putting today's specials on the chalkboard," Sara added with pleasure in her handiwork.

"Lookin' good, Sara."

Two cops from the nearby precinct came in with their order of black coffee and fried eggs on a roll. Cora went over to the counter to greet them by name. A changing ensemble of regulars showed up at the Athena at all hours. The station house stood only a few blocks away, and the diner was known for its strong, agreeable coffee. Over time a few officers had become more friends than customers. And if Cora ever needed any sort of help most of these local cops were glad to offer it. It proved to be mutually beneficial. Cora had a finger on the pulse of the community. Detectives Frank Reynolds and Jonah Hunter especially had more than once given her a hand in some of her off-duty needs and activities. And it was rumored that Detective Jonah Hunter had more than a passing interest in the Athena's striking owner.

Locals began to saunter into the diner, one and two at a time. Everything was arranged, from the utensils to the toilet paper. The lighting was right, the atmosphere cheerful. The Athena Diner ensured that customers had a good amount of space between them. There were paintings along the walls, colorful landscapes of quaint Greek villages and fishing ports. Sara Sweeny, comely in her black outfit, served as hostess this morning, greeting each patron pleasantly. Laminated menus in hand, she escorted them along the row of booths by the windows or to the larger tables around the far side of the counter. The hum of conversation blended with pleasant, soft overhead music. Most of the customers were regulars, with some coming daily. A considerable number were retired, older and elderly working-class people living in this very working-class neighborhood. Others were area businessmen and women, also locals, together with salespeople from the many shops lining the streets. A relaxed environment for everybody.

"Eggs over easy," someone called into the kitchen as they handed over the written ticket.

"I need a small Greek salad. Coffee with half-and-half on the side." requested a waiter with ticket in hand. The busboy, Santiago, hurried over to serve the fresh coffee, filling the empty cup to the brim. The strong satisfying aroma of sweet caramel dissipating in the air pleased the customer.

Cora looked on with approval. She knew Gus would be pleased if he could see her now. More than pleased. He would beam. He'd taught her so much during those early years. Everything about everything. He was missed for sure. She sighed with regret.

The sun rose higher, morning light streamed brightly. In her mind she could envision Gus standing right there, his heavy hands on his hips with his infectious laughter. He was always good-naturedly teasing her as he slowly explained the minutest details of how the diner must operate.

Her English had been good back then, but the world of the strange American diner was new, and restaurant jargon was almost another language. Gus was always careful not to overwhelm her, his young Greek guest, so recently arrived in America. He was a big strong man with calloused hands, a loud and sometimes thunderous tone, but never intimidating with her. No, not with Cora. He treated her gently and with sympathy. Staff took notice of his behavior, especially the way he looked at her, and it became widely whispered, that the burly, demanding owner, Gus Padnos, had fallen in love. His huge heart thumped from the moment he first saw the tall slender girl distant relatives had placed in his care. The extended family had told him everything he needed to know regarding her past life, and the grief she'd endured. They had also spoken a bit about the American diplomat she had once known. So sad. So painful. However, all that was finished. All hands were washed clean of it. Now was a blank slate; she was here in New York, and so was he. Gus himself was a widower two decades older than Cora, who'd been married to a distant cousin. Age wouldn't make a difference. One day, Gus believed and assured himself, perhaps with divine help, the charming girl would accept his optimistic offer and they would be married.

The phones started ringing again. More rush orders for breakfast to go. Foot traffic in the street increased, the unruly noise from the El trains rose and diminished unabated, constantly interrupting conversations. Rush hour in the city, trains and buses and cars all making haste.

"Hey there, Mrs. Gus." Sitting at the counter, coffee mug in hand, Vic Barazas waved a big hello with his broad almost toothless grin. Cora greeted him back. "Hey, Vic. Good morning." Vic had been an addict for many years, now reformed. In recent times he even helped take care of the neighborhood community garden, a communal effort a handful of residents had set up on a small vacant lot. Vic also seemed to know something about everyone and everything going on.

In the far corner booth, Cora noticed a lonely figure with cropped silvery hair sitting and sipping her cup of coffee, hunched over, playing with her cell phone.

"Kind of early for you, Lillian," Cora said, casually walking over to greet her.

The thin older woman looked up with a gentle smile. Her arthritic hands tightly held her cup. The knobby fingers had a slight tremble. "Oh, it's so good to see you, Mrs. Gus. I need a little of your time."

Cora kept her smile even though it was sadly noticeable that Lillian Gorman did not look her chipper self. "How is everything?"

Lillian shrugged. It was regrettably obvious she was in some sort of discomfort. Her old-fashioned thick glasses magnified her bloodshot green eyes and the dark shadows surrounding them. "All these medications again. I'm going back to my doctor tomorrow. This time for my ankles. They've been swelling again. Damn, I don't know how many pills I've already taken this morning. Nothing seems to work quite right these days."

Lilian Gorman had been a long-standing customer at the diner, going back to the time of Gus. Her apartment was barely two streets away, near the basketball court. She had become a steady face for dinner and sometimes lunch. Not often breakfast. "What are you having with your coffee?"

"Oh, I don't feel hungry today." After a swift glance she looked down, clearing her throat, then looked directly into Mrs. Gus's eyes. "I decided to come early this morning to see if I could have a few minutes of your time. When you can spare it. I know how busy you are in the mornings, and I really don't mean to bother. But I have awful news to tell you about what happened with the homeless man." Her voice lowered with worry.

"Who? Which guy do you mean?"

"The one who hangs out down the block. He was all but killed a few nights ago. Left bleeding, lying in the gutter. You haven't heard anything?"

"Not a thing, but I want to hear what happened. Stay where you are, Lillian. Please give me a few minutes." Glancing over her shoulder she saw additional customers lining up to order breakfast. "I'll be back as fast as I can, okay? Then we'll sit together and have a talk about what happened."

Her customer was clearly appreciative. "Thank you, Mrs. Gus. I can sit and wait till you're free." Her brow furrowed. "But if you need this booth for customers…"

"No, no. Don't move an inch, Lillian. I'll be right back."

Cora had earned a reputation as a trustworthy listener, and especially as an asset to those in need. Often neighborhood people sought her for help in all sorts of difficulties. Sometimes it seemed the diner's busy owner spent more time advising others than in operating the Athena Diner. Only a select few of her staff were aware of the extent her private activities. Some called it investigative work, conducting inquiries, or even referred to her as a part-time amateur sleuth. Whichever, she had proved her worth.

The busy register rang and rang. Orders for delivery came in one after the other. The counter filled with patrons dressed for work, soft pop music played on small speakers hung above. Cora felt a growing concern. Left bloody in the gutter, Lillian had said. The thought made her shudder.

Outside, a few clouds gathered and crossed over the sky. Traffic increased, and so did the accompanying noise. The express El trains rumbled towards downtown.

A homeless man being nearly killed mere steps away from her diner. She couldn't shake the notion.

For the Athena Diner another New York day had begun.

And for Cora Drakos it jarred other troubling memories of home.

2

A WARM MORNING NEAR PIRAEUS, the port of Athens. The small bedroom window allowed a glimpse of the land bridge connecting the renowned port to the city. From the hill of *Kastella* pleasant breezes rustled the thin white curtains, allowing a sweeping view over the Athens Basin and Saronic Gulf. Noise from morning traffic rose from nearby narrow streets, and loud drilling of jackhammers doing road repair in the distance grew irritating. The dense urban metropolis had awakened, terracotta clay tile roofs bright in warm morning sunshine. The streets were still wet from the night's rain. Cora had been awake for almost an hour, sitting up, watching the sun rise and a hazy gray sky brighten into a brilliant blue hue. She squinted to bring objects into clearer focus; the city was rapidly growing with dense sprawl spiraling in all directions, an indication that the ailing economy was decisively bouncing back after its long difficult years caused by the difficult recession.

Resting beside her, Dirk Bonneau squirmed and gradually opened his eyes. "How long have you been up?" he asked.

She massaged his shoulder with her hands. "For a while now. I kept quiet because I didn't want to wake you."

He smiled. "You didn't have to do that. But first," he continued, giving her a quick kiss, "I have to use the bathroom." He pushed the sheet aside and effortlessly slid off the bed. Cora's eyes followed him, admiring his brisk movements, and youthful, strong, tanned physique. A magazine image of a healthy male of thirty.

It had been little more than a year since they had first met. She had been working as an assistant to the deputy director at the American Embassy for almost three years, a senior part of the multilingual clerical staff proficient in English as well as Russian. Her comprehension of Russian was good, but she particularly excelled in English, and often was needed to utilize her skills as an interpreter. Dirk Bonneau had been named a political aide to the ambassador, coming directly from Washington, D.C. A mid-level State Department entry replacing a retiring life-long diplomat. Dirk was clearly a smart and ambitious young man of thirty or so. Lean and tall, he seemed a cinema-like character to her. Often during various daily duties, he personally handed her assorted classified documents to remit, confidential security folders to keep safe, people to inform of his numerous out-of-the-office assignments. He joked and chatted with her, sometimes complimenting her dress or her hair. Always polite, always soft spoken. She liked him right away and was not surprised when after a few months he invited her to join him at an official ambassadorial function. Work related, he claimed with his charming smile. Numerous Greek government ministers and dignitaries would be present, and he would love having her at his side, mainly to help with translation when needed. Ambassador Mary Underwood knew of it and approved. He readily admitted his own studies of the Greek language were seriously lacking. Worse than poor, in fact. During his last post which had been in Bucharest he'd fared little better. She liked his easy ability to laugh at himself.

Cora politely accepted his invitation in a professional manner, although a few of her Greek colleagues smiled and predicted he would sooner than later ask her out again. That evening went well; she enjoyed being in his cheerful company and listening to his skillful conversation, rarely needing to translate at all. She also felt certain she would see him again away from work, and next time would be in a more personal setting. Within a week he did ask her out for supper. And although private relationships between midlevel diplomats and trained local staff working for the embassy was not strictly forbidden, it was not encouraged and sometimes even frowned upon.

In the beginning they remained discreet. They met at a nearby gym several times a week after work, then shared meals at popular, quiet restaurants. Soon that was followed by special reservations at the restaurant atop Mount Lycabettus, the highest point in the center of Athens, where they enjoyed a panoramic view of virtually the entire city, lit up at night like golden adornments. Other times they climbed the rock steps of the restoration of the beloved ancient Parthenon, built by Pericles, sitting high atop a compound of temples known as the Acropolis. Dedicated to the goddess Athena, the daughter of Zeus, and protector of the city, with a spear and a shield in her hand, upon it the head of Medusa. A shrine within the Parthenon had originally housed an extraordinary statue of Athena, thought to have stood twelve meters high, known in antiquity as Athena Parthenos. The Parthenon itself had been the center of religious life in the powerful Greek City-State of Athens, forever a symbol of its might, wealth, and gloried culture. Seeing the remains of this cradle of Western civilization now was awe-inspiring for almost every traveler. Dirk marveled at the sights.

Cora was familiar with the area called *Exarhia*, a desirable close-in district just outside the city's center, and close to the university. She was proud to show off Greece's ancient capital of inexpressible magic, and Dirk found himself wide-eyed, and deeply eager to explore the spectacle of the wondrous birthplace of democracy. In her enthusiastic, soft voice she wove for him age-old tales, myths of the gods, tragedies, and betrayals. They strolled through the ruins of the colossal temple of Olympian Zeus, king of all ancient gods. Narratives of his exploits told and retold long before the birth of even antique Rome.

The couple traveled across the hectic central streets in trams and buses, but she repeatedly brought him to the National Garden in the center of the city, commissioned by Amalia, the first Queen of modern Greece. A haven behind the Greek Parliament building where they could walk freely, adorned by hundreds of different plants and trees collected from all over the world, wander up and down the lovely, serene green trails, and endless winding and flowered pathways. The *Planka* neighborhood, narrow with its tight clusters of shops, colorful churches, restaurants, and celebrated bazaars daily patronized by locals and foreigners alike. The Ancient Agora, and the Roman Agora. Dirk Bonneau found himself overwhelmed in this classic nirvana, captivated by both Athens and his charismatic guide.

They toured the grand museums, considered among the finest in the world. The wondrous Cycladic Art Museum bursting with marble sculpture, and the Acropolis Museum, equally astounding, bringing back to life the days of Athens during the height of its majesty. Beneath the Acropolis were found the ongoing excavations, ever discovering more of the surviving splendor of Athenian history. The mesmerizing famous names learned in schools across the world, all native to this place, Aristotle, Plato, Socrates. Dirk was offered an endless account of the exalted past, and the center beginnings of today's western world as we know it. Athens proved to be a stunning tableau, and he realized that now he had become a part of it. Art, culture, beauty, were everywhere to be found. Amazingly, even within numerous Metro underground stations, statues, busts and artworks stood proudly on display for all to admire.

Before long Cora and Dirk found themselves holding hands as they continued to ramble through the city. Neither thought how strong or deep the relationship might grow. Nor how quickly.

Invited to the family home for dinner, Dirk met her whole family several times. He easily charmed her mother, Annella, and especially Lyra, Cora's older sister, if not her cautious businesslike father, Zander Drakos, a successful man dealing in the import and export trade. Yet even this hardened, alert well-heeled businessman recognized that the fascinating American and his daughter had the makings of a good couple. Soon, both relatives and friends incessantly speculated not whether but when the couple might make an announcement of their intention to wed. Dirk's assignment was scheduled to keep him in Greece for several more years, although the number of sudden short trips he was being sent on increased. At times Cora began to wonder if there was something more to his work than his official title called for.

"How long do you expect to be gone?" she asked as he eased himself back into bed. He pulled her closer. "Four days max," he said with a frown. "It'll go fast."

"Oh. When will you be leaving this time?"

He wavered before answering. "Unfortunately, I have to leave tonight." For him this was routine business, often important. Yet it seemed odd to her. These frequent excursions weren't typical of other diplomats at the embassy.

"Can you tell me where they're sending you?"

"Of course. Istanbul again."

She nodded, pleased with the destination. At least there weren't all these anti-American demonstrations going on there now. He had been sent to the prominent Turkish city several times in recent months. A positive change in relations between America and Turkey might be brewing, she knew. "I'll never understand why they keep using you as some sort of courier. A common messenger could do the job as well. They could have practically anyone at the embassy act as courier. Why use someone in your capacity, Mr. Political Assistant Deputy?"

"It's all part of my paygrade, *akgrivos*." He used the endearing Greek word for beloved. "My parents I could disobey, Ambassador Mary Underwood I can't. You know what they say in the military: The man says 'frog' and I gotta jump. That's just the way it is."

"Don't try to shut me up with your boyish charm." She sat up straight, her naked back against the headboard, bare breasts firm. She waited for him to say something. He didn't. Dirk was quite adept at avoiding her scrutiny.

"You know, when you first arrived at your embassy appointment, I checked you out very carefully on my computer. All strictly confidential information according to Washington regarding your last evaluation." He stared at her quizzical smile. "We Greeks always like to check out new residents," she added with a poke. "We feel entitled to know what we're being sent."

"Hmm. Maybe you shouldn't have received that classification upgrade promotion, Cora Drakos. Well, don't hold back. What did you discover? Secret agent stuff you read in some Russian documents you translated? My name on a cloak-and-dagger watch list? Suspected of double agent spying for the Russians, or maybe China?" He chuckled and put his head on her lap, eyes gazing up into hers. She huffed and turned her head away. There was always a bit of wildness about her that he adored. "Did this dossier about me mention a reason for taking a post in Athens, requiring that I find myself a beautiful woman…but I wound up settling for you?" He laughed.

She took a pillow and tried to stuff the edge of it into his mouth. Then they laughed together. After that they made love. Cora had much more interesting things to think about than schedules.

The next morning Cora was off from work, so she, her sister Lyra and Lyra's daughter went grocery shopping. Returning to Lyra's home, nine-year-old Thea fell asleep in front of the television. Lyra poured coffee and served fresh *kouloura*, bagel-shaped sesame bread rings, and they relaxed together on the terrace.

"It's good spending time together," said Lyra, sinking far back into her plush chair, kicking off her high heels, putting tired feet up on the ottoman. "You've been so busy, hardly even returning calls. None of the family has seen you lately. Mama's wondering about you, but we all know how she can be."

"Always a mother hen. Did you ever think she'd ever change?"

They both laughed. As Lyra poured more coffee, Cora sat still, sunglasses on, legs splayed outward, soaking up sun. Lyra observed her closely. Her younger sister appeared restless again, distracted. It was happening a lot recently. She knew Cora better than anyone, and it was evident something wasn't quite right. "Let's hear it, little sister. Spit it out. All of it."

"I know I haven't been much fun lately. I apologize. These days my entire world has become so hectic. I can hardly keep track of anything. Long days at work, late nights."

"You mean late nights with Dirk? Ah, I see. Perhaps this has something due to pangs of young love?"

Cora groaned at the weak attempt at humor. "Seeing you're asking, I guess you could surmise Dirk probably plays a part in everything."

Lyra pressed on. "Why don't you just tell me what's taking place in that scheming clever head of yours. Is something the matter? You did sound agitated on the phone."

"Did I?" Cora tried to brush it off. "Work is fine, fascinating, and intense as always. These crazy Americans. Our Ambassador Underwood is going to be attending a big meeting in Paris soon. Part of a routine NATO gathering. But the way Dirk's been managing his part you'd think he's accompanying the president for caviar in the Kremlin or something."

"Isn't that part of his job? You haven't mentioned a word at all about anything personal. How is your private life with him? Looking forward to a wedding soon? Even Papa has accepted him as a soon-to-be member of the family."

Cora avoided here sister's gaze. "Things with Dirk are good too. We are planning to wed. No date set yet. Perhaps after the summer." She stopped, then said, "But..."

"But what?"

Her brows tightened and she thought for a while before answering. "I know it probably doesn't make any sense, but I keep getting these odd feelings I can't shake off," Cora admitted. Then she dropped her eyes and studied her nails, sorry she had brought it up.

"What sort of feelings?" Lyra prompted after a long silence.

Cora leaned in closer, her hands folded on her lap. Her plate was hardly touched, only a single bite taken out of the *kouloura*. "Nothing I can really explain. Call it intuition. I've been feeling edgy. He's always on call. Day or night. No other Americans of his grade get dispatched the way he does. It might happen to be ranking staff occasionally. With Dirk, though... Currently, it's like he's here, then he goes, then he's back, then a few weeks later off he goes again. No planning, no preparation, no notice. A phone call and a plane ticket. And with all the protests everywhere against America, it makes me uncomfortable. When I heard that terrorists had kidnapped those missionaries it only added to my fears."

Lyra considered herself a down-to-earth, pragmatic person. Cora's complaint seemed authentic given the political upheaval in the world today, but was that really the core of her worry? Perhaps Cora was becoming nervous about committing herself for the first time to one man, and a foreigner at that. At the moment, she appeared most unlike the brilliant, poised young woman she had proven herself to be at university and then at her translator's job. Lyra said gently, "He's a diplomat. They follow orders. That's what they're paid to do, isn't it?"

Cora nodded. "Yes, but..." She waved one slim hand as if to swat a fly. "He doesn't talk much about these trips. And he's always guarded if I ask questions. Too many questions, he tells me. Sometimes he makes jokes about my asking him anything at all." Her words trailed off.

"Wait a minute, Cora. He's not permitted to give details, right? Keeping government affairs confidential, isn't that part of a diplomat's job? Look at Papa and how he oversees business dealings. Especially with those export dealings." Lyra spoke in a wry pitch. "Papa's shrewder than a Persian carpet seller. He wines and dines his clients like they're royalty. Then by the time he's finished they think they're getting the bargain of the century. And we know Papa doesn't discuss trade details with anyone, ever. Not even Mama. It's all hush-hush trading, totally confidential. To Papa, business is considered top secret. You know that. And who knows who Papa meets up with in these private meetings he attends? In my view, Dirk is just trying to take advantage of any opportunity to advance his career, so he volunteers for assignments that make him look good to his superiors. Also, maybe to impress higher up state department big shots in Washington. It sounds to me like he's trying to get noticed. Wanting to make his name stand out. I like that your man is being very professional."

"I know you're probably right. I'm being foolish. But I can't shake this concern …" Here she paused. "The honest truth is I'm feeling really worried."

Lyra's eyes widened. She put down her cup of tea. "All right. Spell it out for me. You're having some serious doubts? You think there might be some other woman? Suspicion he's hiding too many things from you?"

Cora felt foolish as her sister chided her. She placed down her cup and tea splashed over the rim. While she wiped the mess Cora reached for the right words to explain better how she felt. Finally, she said, "Call it a sour feeling, in my gut. Since I've been working closely with these Americans I've gotten to know and understand them quite well. Naturally, they take their duties seriously. Everyone working at the embassy knows and understands there are matters never to speak of. Government secrets and undisclosed plans. But not everything is always restricted. After hours you'd be surprised; even top officials start to relax, open up a little. Everything happening in the world isn't grim and dangerous. They all find time to chat, have a few drinks after hours, laugh, sometimes even gossip and flirt."

Lyra made a face. She considered herself to be a levelheaded, worldly woman. "You've already confronted Dirk, you told me. You've let him know how this is troubling you, even making you question things…" It was less a question than a statement.

"Of course, I've done all that. More than once. But he's so damn quick to come up with a story or two that explains it all away. I've come to believe he makes things up just to try and please me."

Lyra leaned over and squeezed Cora's hand. "All right then. Go get drunk. Both of you. Ply him with ouzo. Be indispensable, take off your clothes and seduce him like never before. Then when he's worn out and dead asleep go through his wallet, his pockets. Look for tickets, rentals, any time-stamped proof of where he's been or going." She couldn't help but break into loud laughter. "Oh heaven, if only my own marriage was so good."

Tensions broke. Cora found herself laughing along with her sister. Lyra had been having her own issues at home for a while now. With her daughter in the next room this wasn't a suitable time to broach them.

"My advice, Cora," Lyra said when the laughter subsided. "Don't be so dramatic. You'll learn Dirk has his reasons, whatever they are. Trust him—at least for the time being. He deserves that much, doesn't he? It's clear to everyone I know how he feels about you." She kept her grin, and she was glad to see her sister finally be to relax. "So, tell me, when will your devious American be returning this time?"

"Sunday."

"Only a few days from now. I'll wager he'll be more than happy to see you at the door. And the same goes for you seeing him. I can already hear the two of you going at it in the middle of the night." Lyra raised her eyebrows, and her eyes danced with a twinkle. They laughed together again. "Ah, the mysteries of life. Just wait, little sister. You'll discover I'm right."

And she did have a valid point, Cora acknowledged. Perhaps there was a bit of jealousy she was nurturing regarding some secret life Dirk was hiding away in a closet.

After a pause, she muttered, "You obviously have all of life's mysteries solved better than I do. I guess you win this time, big sister." Quickly adding, "but I still have qualms."

3

THE DINER WAS BUSIER THAN usual for an early spring day. "Mrs. Gus!" Her name rang out in an endless procession of work-related questions from the staff. The morning delivery driver was standing outside, rightly being dressed down by Eddie Coltrane. Cora answered everything she was asked deftly, momentarily watching her new manager with satisfaction, glad she had given the right man the position. She slowly made her way back to the booth where Lillian Gorman had been sitting for an hour, patiently waiting.

She slid in opposite, exhaling loudly, and giving the older woman a sincere smile. "So, Lillian, what on earth is going on?"

Before she could reply, the busboy Santiago filled the coffee cup to the brim. Lillian gladly accepted a fresh brew.

Her visit today made her distraught. "I was hoping you might have had a few answers, Mrs. Gus. Where are the police when you need them?" Her tone turned even more dour; her eyes glanced at nearby tables and customers, as if to check if they were eavesdropping.

Lillian was having difficulty in finding suitable words. At length she began talking in a muffled voice. "The man I mentioned. The one always sitting on a wooden box down the street. You know who I mean. You've noticed him too."

"The homeless guy on the next corner, right? The one who's always wearing an old baseball cap pulled down low?"

She nodded emphatically. "Yes, that's him. You do know who I mean, thank heaven. He never bothers anyone. Never asks for anything, but there's always a small container right beside him. Sometimes I toss in a few coins."

"Sure, I'm aware of him. He's been a familiar face around here for a while. Occasionally he ventures into the diner to get a cup of coffee to go."

"But he only comes in when it's quiet, right? He never disturbs or looks for trouble, does he?"

"Not at all. He's the quiet type, not a loudmouth. We give him a few sandwiches, a large coffee to go. He insists on paying something. He pulls some coins from his pocket or tries to leave a dollar. I've instructed Sara and the other cashiers not to take it. Or quietly slip the money back into his pocket. I feel bad for him. He's not the troublemaking kind. As far as I know the cops leave him alone. I know he drinks, but he doesn't cause concern. I think everyone knows he's not a danger to anyone except maybe to himself." She looked out the window beyond the traffic, to the place at the opposite corner where this unfortunate man usually positioned himself. "Come to think of it, Lillian, I don't recall seeing him for a while. Probably at least week."

Lillian nodded. Cora noticed that her knobby hands were unsteady with nervous emotion. "Do you know him, Lillian? I mean personally know him?"

Lillian Gorman drew a deep breath. "I wish I didn't have to say this. I… He wasn't there at all last week. Usually when I'm out grocery shopping, he asks if I need help carrying my bags. I say yes sometimes. I let him hold one or two bags, and then give him a few dollars as a tip. Maybe that keeps him from a soup kitchen that night Other times I've notice him standing by the corner, telling the kids when the light changes, and when it's okay to cross the street. He even escorts the little kids from time to time."

"I've noticed he does that too. He's a real character. He seems to genuinely like kids. You don't suspect…?"

"Oh no, Mrs. Gus! Nothing like that." She shook her head vehemently, silver hair falling over her forehead. "He's just trying to be helpful, not to feel useless, I suppose. I've always felt pity for him. But now after this…" A brief pained expression flashed over her face. She regained her composure, waiting to hear more of Cora's thoughts. Cora looked long and hard at her aging companion. Barely perceptible tears were forming in the corners of her bloodshot tired eyes. Lillian Gorman had clearly been more concerned than she was letting on.

"What is it, Lillian? You can be honest with me." Inquisitive, she stretched an earnest hand and held onto Lillian's in an offer of reassurance.

Lillian's voice became little more than a whisper. "I found out he's been taken to the hospital. He was beat up one-night last week. No one saw anything. Maybe he got some punks or druggies angry. Maybe a gang hurt him just for kicks. Whatever happened, they beat him viciously, breaking some ribs, smashed him in the face. He had a concussion." Here she paused. "I found out one of his eyes were damaged."

"Where did you learn all that? You were looking to me for news."

Traffic began to honk at a stalled bus outside. "I heard it last night," she admitted. "On my way home, I ran into that nighttime police sergeant."

"Molina?"

She nodded. "Yes, Molina. He was sitting in his patrol car eating a sandwich, right in front of my building. He's a nice man. Doing rounds, or on the way back to the precinct, I gather. Molina nodded hello to me, and I stopped by his car and asked if he knew where the homeless man was. It seemed so strange that the guy wasn't hanging around anymore. Not after being here for so long. Molina dithered about revealing anything to me. I don't think he was supposed to say a word, but I bothered him. I told him I was concerned, and that I often tried to be helpful to the poor guy. So, he quietly told me a few things. It happened during the middle of a night last week, while he was huddling in some doorway around the corner, trying to keep out of the rain. Remember the big thunderstorms we had? Molina didn't know what started the fight or why, but it was over fast. There were a few shouts, then cries, and Molina said a patrol car with flashing lights reached the scene. Its siren probably broke things up. The attacker fled, and the cops found the homeless man bleeding in the wet street, unconscious."

Mrs. Gus was truly shocked by all this.

"The cops called an ambulance," Lillian continued, "and EMS came and took him away. I have no idea if he was stabbed or whatever, what or why. Only that was beaten badly. Or worse. For what reason, who knows? Maybe they even wanted to kill him. But if he is alive and recovering, I'd like to learn about it, find out to see if I can offer some help. Poor man." There was a plea now in her eyes, "But I don't even know his name. Just another poor lost soul..."

"He calls himself Matt or Mitch," Cora said trying to recall. "I asked him his name a long time ago. "He was hesitant about giving it. Matt or Mitch, I'm fairly sure. But he didn't offer me a last name. It was the night of the blackout."

A memorable night never forgotten. Large swaths of the city were virtually shut down, no streetlights, and more than half the population huddled without power. Due to a substation explosion, it was being reported. People were in a panic. The diner's backup generator kept the refrigerators cold, and the lights dimmed, but at least we managed to remain open. The Athena Diner became a beacon in the dark. Cora made sure cold drinks were given out to passersby, mostly neighborhood folks gathering in the streets in the summer heat. Traffic lights were out or blinking uselessly. Cora recalled the homeless man helping several people get safely across the streets while avoiding slow moving traffic and copious honking horns. Reflections from headlights highlighted his disheveled, badly worn old clothes. His normally haggard and sad face held an infrequent look of dignity on that particular occasion. It appeared to Cora that he was pleased to be of assistance to people for once.

That night it took long, difficult hours until electricity was finally restored, neighborhood by neighborhood. Everyone was exhausted. The homeless guy sat himself down against a brick wall across the street, totally fatigued. He also appeared to be in pain. Cora remembered that she hurriedly brought him a couple of cold cut sandwiches and two large bottles of water. He'd looked up at her with forlorn, but grateful eyes. She asked him his name. He muttered it softly and thanked her. She recalled those bloodshot eyes being wide and expressive. He didn't drink any booze that night. He may be destitute, but he gave her the impression of being someone able to survive another day on New York's harsh streets.

As he eagerly drank his chilly water she quietly walked away, leaving him alone to return to his world.

"Matt, yes." Lillian repeated as though she were remembering something. She bit at her lower lip. "I just wanted to tell you what I heard. It's awful, isn't it? I wondered if perhaps you'd heard anything new?" She sat with her thin shoulders sagging. Poor Lillian appeared anxious. Even a little frightened.

"What can I do for you, Lillian? What are you asking from me?"

"You know so many people…you have a way of…finding things out. I know that people come to you sometimes, and you try to help…Like what happened with those drug dealers a couple of years back. They say you had a lot to do with getting them off our streets."

"Now you're flattering me, Lillian." It was an episode that brought unwelcome attention to the local area. Word on the street was that nearby neighborhood gangs had brought low level dealers selling hard stuff at night along several thoroughfares. It started with loitering, then an increase in suspicious traffic, and scattered hypodermic needles. Next followed car theft. More undesirable traffic, distributing, and soon street crime alarmingly increased. People in the neighborhood were becoming alarmed, and the community was suffering. An exodus of business was feared.

Quietly in her clandestine way Mrs. Gus had begun monitoring the comings and goings of these drug dealers. It was easy enough having the cops get junkies busted, but beyond that she was determined to reach bigger game: climbing the chain to the dealer's key suppliers. Slyly using contact acquaintances said to be members of organized crime, she was able to trace the main distributor. Shortly, one dealer mysteriously disappeared. It was rumored he was dead, and now the game began to change. Mrs. Gus made certain the rumor went viral. Maybe it was true and maybe it wasn't—but other low-level dealers were becoming increasingly uneasy. Police vigilance increased. And soon after, an influential informant threw the whole operation into upheaval. Numerous arrests ensued, including a massive bust of the principal supplier in Brooklyn. Deal pleading led to more investigations, some believed still ongoing. And just as suddenly as the street dealing had begun, it abruptly ended. Dealing anywhere remotely near the diner had become bad for business. Keeping her hands and name out of it, Cora had been very much involved. No one knew for sure, but many were certain she had played a decisive role.

"All I did was complain to the police. It was bad for business. Not just mine. You're giving me credit I don't deserve, Lillian."

"No, I didn't mean it that way, Mrs. Gus. Everybody mentions you have good connections. Not only with the cops, but businesses and politicians, and almost everything that goes on around here."

Cora chuckled. "I still think you're giving me far too much recognition."

"Okay. Let's say I'm hoping you might be able to get information about what happened to that poor homeless man. Putting two and two together and," she paused, "learning his condition and where he is now. If he'd been drinking that night, it could have made things worse. I mean, he wouldn't have had a chance to defend himself, or been able. They even could have shot him."

The echo of a faraway memory shook Cora. Gunshots. Deadly bullets. She tried to erase it from her mind, without success. That was a distant time, a forgotten world in Athens, she reminded herself. After a moment's pause, she said, "So, you'd like me to make some enquiries for you?"

Lillian looked pleased. "Oh yes, if you would. Thank you. I know you're swamped with other problems. And this is a tough time." The buzz of the diner filled their ears. "But I already feel so much better, Mrs. Gus. I do. Just knowing that you'll ask around and do what you can."

"Does Venice have gondolas? You have my word, Lillian. I'll keep you informed on whatever I find out."

Cora drew a deep breath. The night was cooler and humid. She walked down the darkened street, winding her way home. It had been a long day. Lights were out in the Athena Diner, floors mopped, tables reset, the diner finally closed shut for the night. It loomed over its corner location like a hulking giant. Scrubbed and cleaned, tables set up and prepared for the next morning, garbage bagged high into dumpsters in the back, ready to be picked up by private sanitation before dawn.

"Hey, Mrs. Gus." Came a voice from the shadows.

She turned sideways. It was Julio, a nice local teen known for always ordering his burgers very, very well done. Some had dubbed him as the Burn Burger Boy as a nickname. "Hey Julio," she answered back with a small wave. The kid grinned and walked in the opposite direction. It felt like every single person this side of Jamaica Avenue knew her.

She was feeling tired and looking forward to catching some needed sleep. However, her thoughts skittered over demands at the diner, and finally reaching home in her apartment she found herself mulling over Lillian Gorman. The Athena could take care of itself, a feat she had accomplished by hard training of her best people, like Eddie and assistant manager Wally. Lillian, though, appeared to be a melancholy lonely lady living by herself in a tiny apartment since her invalid mother and then husband passed away. She had known Lillian as a patron for some years. She always arrived by herself, sitting at a small table near the back. Usually, she would read or spend time looking at her phone. Never getting involved with other regulars who enjoyed treating the Athena as their favorite hangout. Sometimes she'd be there for lunch, sometimes for dinner too. Why all the interest in this homeless man? she wondered. True, it was tragic the way he had been beaten. He certainly didn't deserve that.

Perhaps it would be a good idea to stop by the precinct and check in with her friend Jonah Hunter tomorrow. The streetwise detective had a good handle on local events. Beyond that, Hunter had become a trusted confidante. A two-way street that proved mutually advantageous. How odd it must be for a detective to carry a last name like Hunter, she thought. How many snide comments or the butt of wiseass jokes had he endured? Cora allowed herself a small smirk at the thought and became drowsy.

She tossed and turned long into the night, unable to sleep soundly. She read for a while, got up, stared from the window. Nothing helped. Sleep remained elusive. Her thoughts threw her back several decades, back to the world she grew up in. The old world she couldn't forget as much as she tried.

And again, her mind summoned up that one singular night, so often repeated in nightmares. In it she was alone, frightened, trying to steady shaky hands. She was sweating, heart thumping in her chest, muscles in her gut painfully cramped. Holding her breath, she inched forward inside the cavernous, dilapidated warehouse, carefully making her way between hazardously piled stacks of worn wooden crates, pallets, and boxes scattered in long haphazard rows. Above, the ceiling panels were dislodged and loose, suspended here and there at odd angles. The odor inside the depository was foul with urine and animal droppings.

Rising putridly from another aisle came a sickly-sweet stench of something decayed, something dead. Dusky light seeped through a series of sooty, cracked windows encased in years of grime. She caught a glimpse of a mouse darting amid the shadows. This place was infested. Were there rats too? The thought of rodents hiding among the crates made her shudder. This bleak warehouse wasn't far from the old wharf at the western edge, far from the new main terminal, embedded in a complex of old stone warehouses built during a much earlier period of challenging times in the long life of Piraeus. Once this building had been a busy, thriving storage facility. Now it stood moribund, a pitiful remnant of a struggling time.

Merchant marine boats and container ships in the harbor stood anchored nearby, bright lights flashing. There would also be a few police patrols prowling near this place, she knew. She mustn't be seen. No matter what. No one must ever learn of her business here.

She felt for the flashlight tucked into her back pocket. Feeling it there gave her a modicum of reassurance. She knew she would need it soon.

She had been warned this place was considered dangerous. To keep far away. Drug addicts came here to hide, someone at the embassy warned. Underworld related gang members brought victims here, others conjectured. Victims as doomed as this place itself. The building had long been condemned. Government planners perpetually waited for the go-ahead from bureaucrats to have it demolished, part of a planned industrial renewal. Somehow that never seemed to happen with this hulking, time-worn blight.

Cora moved steadily down the widest aisle. She turned at the abrupt sound of a low whistle. It repeated. Someone was standing at the distant end, across from a cluster of piled boxes stacked high in a far corner. She strained to see, moved closer to the sound. Her contact held up his cell phone to provide her with a moment of light. She breathed in and out deeply, slowly, in a calming meditation.

"You have the money? As agreed?" The voice was thickly accented, low, and guttural, with a strong masculine trait. He wore a dark jacket with the collar pulled up high around his neck. Shadow hid his face except for small slits for eyes and a pinched mouth.

She faced him directly, trying to muster confidence. She cleared her throat and spoke in a firm voice. "I have it. Precisely as was agreed."

He held out a gloved hand. He was careful, not about to leave any trace of fingerprints. "Give it here, eh?" He snapped his gloved fingers. "Let's not waste either of our time."

She wavered momentarily.

"You don't have to be afraid. If I wanted to hurt you, I would have already. So, let's not play games."

Carefully, she drew a folded envelope from under her sweater. "The information we discussed," she hissed. "Full name, whereabouts, street address, flat number. I want it all. That was my arrangement with your friend."

"I have it here. Everything you required. A deal is a deal. My package has all details you requested—and are going to need." He showed her a small leather pouch. "All the information is inside this."

"If you're lying, I'll find you. I know your contacts, your dealings."

His lips drew back into a snarl. "Are you trying to threaten me? Don't bother. My word is good on the street. But you already know that. That's the reason you searched my partner out. That's the reason you're here now." He snapped his fingers. "So enough talking, eh? Hand over the money."

She drew another deep breath and reluctantly handed him the envelope filled with cash. "Ten thousand euros, that was the price."

"That was the price," he repeated, furnishing her with the pouch. It felt heavy. "As I said, everything is inside."

"Aren't you going to count the money?"

He shook his head, frowning, thick fingers squeezing the envelope. "No need. If you shortchanged me, I know how to find you, too." His frown turned into a small grin. "You're asking for trouble with this package you bought. But I think you already know that. Good luck."

She watched as he spun around, ducked between crates, and disappeared into obscurity. She gripped the leather pouch tightly, turned the other way and hurried to get out of that forsaken place as fast as she could manage.

4

JONAH HUNTER LEANED BACK IN his chair and blew on the hot black coffee. Blue eyes shifted as he scanned the detective squad room. He was greeted by a dozen mostly empty chairs at this early hour, disorderly desktops crammed with laptops, desk lights, books, photographs, and other assorted paraphernalia. On the faded green wall opposite an aging sign hung crookedly. 'Don't forget to wear a mask,' it read. 'If you have a fever, report to your supervisor.' He looked sourly at the reminder of the covid pandemic.

"Hey Hunter, you have a visitor."

The detective's attention turned toward the door. A dark-haired attractive woman wearing sunglasses and a colorful scarf around her neck stood patiently beside a uniformed officer. He recognized her right away.

Smiling widely, he stood up and gestured for her to come over and sit down. A female detective nearby glanced and quickly returned to her computer.

"Detective Hunter," Cora greeted with a small smile of her own. "It's been quite a while."

"If I remember right, the last time I saw you was when you brought me info on those gang members we brought in for manslaughter."

"You're right. Rival gangs. Whatever happened with them?"

Hunter raised his brows. "They worked the system. Good lawyers. Judge gave ten years. They'll be out in seven—or less." He offered her coffee.

She turned it down. "How's the diner business? You look good for someone with your crazy schedule. Dawn till midnight."

"Not that bad, but the same as always. It's bedlam. Customers craving food, or company, or just to get outside. Have a place to go, eyeballing a live person to talk with instead of staring at a screen." She took off her sunglasses. Hunter appreciated that she was a very good-looking woman for someone probably close to fifty.

"And customers also come to see you," he added. It was an open secret in the neighborhood that Mrs. Gus was habitually willing to be helpful when needed by assorted acquaintances.

She waved her hand in dismissal. "Oh, that's just gossip. So many of them are lonely, that's all. I give a shoulder to cry on. So many sad people, living alone. It's really a pity. I make sure the Athena provides a safe place. Provide a hot meal they don't have to cook. I'm really just part of the woodwork. But I think you already know all that, Jonah."

"I know that you're the best thing around." He swiveled in his chair. "If there were a local popularity contest, you'd win it hands down." He looked at her with a slight close-lipped smile. "You do know how people refer to the Athena?"

She looked back without answering.

"They say it's the diner of lost souls."

"Ha." That nickname was certainly nothing she hadn't heard, so she didn't bother responding. "As a matter of fact, though, you might say the Athena's nickname is the reason I came by to see you today,"

"Oh, this visit isn't to finally arrange for that fancy dinner you've been promising for ages?"

"We'll do that fancy dinner one day soon, Detective. I give you my word." Their eyes met for a moment.

"Okay. I can bide my time. I'm a patient guy. So, tell me, what's it gonna be today, Mrs. Gus? What's going on?"

Again, she laughed. "Cora, my name's Cora. We're not at the restaurant now." She paused momentarily and said,

"One of my regulars who lives a few blocks away asked me if I would check with the police. She's trying to get information. An older lady, who's really been concerned. About a week ago this homeless man who hangs out near the diner was savagely beaten up. He hasn't shown his face around since. No one seems to have any idea what happened. No word on the street either, I'm told. I've asked around. For some reason this regular seems to care about the poor guy. She's afraid he's lying in some hospital somewhere—or maybe worse."

Hunter thought for a moment and nodded. "Yeah, I think heard something about that." He leaned forward and typed on his keyboard. He stared at the screen for a while before clicking on the mouse. "The case is still open, it says. Sergeant Molina's people found the guy near a gutter. As you said, pretty badly beaten, and left bleeding. He might have died if no one had reported him lying there like that. According to the report there are no leads yet."

"You think maybe a gang behind it?"

Hunter was a meticulous cop, lining up his facts. He took his time, then said, "I'd have thought a gang, yeah, but this one doesn't seem to be. There was a witness. I can't tell you the name, but this witness saw most of it from their window right across the way. They reported something that started as a loud argument between the guy and his attacker. Mostly one-sided shouting. It looks like the homeless guy tried to avoid getting into a fight. According to the witness statement it claims he tried to take off fast. Before he had a chance to run, he was assaulted. Pretty damn viciously, our witness reported. Did some real damage. Bones, ribs. It says here he suffered a severe injury to one of his eyes. He's damned lucky our witness didn't hesitate to call 911."

Lillian's evaluation had been correct, Cora realized. She hadn't exaggerated. "Does your report say if he's still in the hospital?"

"Hmm. They wanted to keep him longer, but he declined. Released after an emergency visit overnight. Went right back to the street I suppose, but apparently didn't come back around here. Naturally, we have no address for him. He was offered a bed in a shelter, but he refused that too. Signed himself out at the first opportunity. It's a 'John Doe' case. No real name or identity. But it's going to take a while for him to heal. No wonder he's keeping himself far away from here. I don't blame him."

"And no leads. Then there's nothing at all to go on?"

"Nothing firm at all on him or the offender. Perp reportedly a white male, medium height, seemed well built. And loud. He was screaming savagely at the old guy. The attacker was definitely younger, but not a kid. But it was raining hard, so it's difficult to make out anyone's age from a distance." Hunter puffed his cheeks, kept reading. "Next thing, according to the witness, the perp clutched him and beat him to ground. The witness thinks he maybe swung something. Maybe a club, a small bat, but no weapons were found. Pounded mostly with fists."

Hunter's brows drew together. He shrugged to Cora. "Our victim hadn't been drinking that night, looks like. Not over the limit, according to the alcohol level in his blood. At least that's what the report reads after the ambulance brought him in. Just one hell of a beating. It could have turned into a manslaughter charge. Poor guy. No one deserves that."

"Doesn't it sound odd, Hunter? I mean, why would someone go to so much trouble over a homeless guy? Not for money. Drugs? Or stolen drugs maybe? Think it's possible they knew other?"

Hunter studied the situation. "Sure. I'd agree with that. To take so much time and trouble, I'd say it was sadistic. So, you might be right. But what's the end game here? There would have to be some hell of a powerful motive. But again, I think you're right, this wasn't a typical street robbery."

Cora bit her lip. "How can I find out more?"

"I can do some follow up with the hospital. At least try to find a name of some sort. Homeless types usually don't have valid identification.

Generally, they provide a handy alias. Hence, our 'John Doe.' Sometimes because they're too afraid to say anything, or even let a social worker try to find a decent shelter. It amazes me. Never mind their being entitled to sign up for food stamps, or other kind of benefits available. So, no major surprise this guy avoided whatever help offered. He didn't want anyone to know who he is. It's a strange, weird world they live in on the streets. And it's not getting better."

"Can I get to speak with the social worker involved?"

"Maybe. I can give it a shot. But there are bureaucratic laws preventing them from discussing clients. Privacy issues, blah blah, blah. You know the score. Better if I can track down one of the EMT people who brought him into the hospital. They'd have the initial report from directly at the scene."

"Thanks, Hunter. Any help you can offer would be great. And it might give this lady some peace of mind. I owe you one."

The blue-eyed detective chuckled. "I figure you owe me about ninety-five."

Today was a slower lunch hour. Behind the counter, Selina, a skilled waitress, stood off to the side chatting softly into her phone. Eddie Coltrane was at the back door of the kitchen discussing how he wanted the cook's assistants to handle tonight's dinner crowd. Cora mindlessly stared out the window at the traffic in the street lining up, waiting for the light to turn green. Up the steps and into the diner came a young kid. A quiet eleven-year-old boy who frequently came after school to buy ice cream or maybe have a burger if he had enough money.

Cora eyed him and quickly came over. "Nice to see you again, Tyler. What would you like today?"

The kid looked up with wide eyes. "I think today I'll have a small vanilla cone."

"I'll take care of him, Mrs. Gus," came a voice.

"It's okay, Selina. I'll do it." As she took the scooper and ladled vanilla into the cone, she said, "So Tyler, how's your sister doing? Getting over her bronchitis?"

Tyler nodded. "Yeah. She's been really, really pretty sick. But now she's up and out of bed. All this week, and the doctor says she's ready to go back to school. She bugs me every day when I get home. She's been a real pain in the butt."

Mrs. Gus tried not to smile. "Glad to hear she's on the mend. Please give your family my best wishes. By the way, I was just wondering something else. I think you may remember that poor homeless guy with the baseball cap who's always trying to help kids across the street after school?"

He took the cone and nodded again. "Sure, I do. Nobody really wants his help, but it's like he lives on that corner. Thinks he's in charge. But he doesn't bother anybody if that's what you want to know."

She shook her head. "I didn't think he did. It's just…" she paused "Have you seen this guy around lately?"

Tyler thought briefly. "I heard something bad happened to him. He got pretty badly beat up, someone said at school. But I don't know anything about what happened."

"You know the guy's name?"

He expertly licked a drip off his ice cream cone while shaking his head. "I don't know anything about him--except he's a real strange guy. Mostly my friends laugh at him, making jokes about him hunched over in the morning, sitting there with an empty bottle. Most times you can smell the booze." He snapped his fingers. "I know. Maybe you can ask Ramon Maldonado. He's in a different class. Ball player. He might know something."

"Is that the curly-headed kid with pimples?"

Tyler nodded again. "Yeah. He loves baseball. Likes to show off his muscles, especially to girls. He's always bragging, telling everybody how he plans to turn pro someday." A broad grin crossed Tyler's childlike face.

"But he doesn't impress anybody. Except maybe the homeless guy. I think he knows lots about baseball. When he's not all drunk, he loves to talk about it. Ramon stops and spends a little time with him. I've seen them a few times. I think he's even tried to teach Ramon how to throw a fastball or put better spin on a curveball. Stuff like that."

Mrs. Gus raised her brows and listened with interest. "Do me a favor, Tyler. Ask your friend Ramon to stop by after school tomorrow. I'd really appreciate it. I'd like to hear more."

Tyler gave her a small thumbs up. "No problem, Mrs. Gus. I'll tell him." He reached into his pocket for money to pay for the cone. Cora waved her hand. "It's a freebie today. And for Ramon too if he'll talk some baseball to me."

Ramon Maldonado was a stocky, muscular kid, tall for his twelve years, with thick lips and thicker eyebrows. He stood straight, his broad shoulders and compact arms a clear sign he was someone you wouldn't want to confront in a physical fight. At first glance he appeared far older than someone not quite thirteen. His small narrow eyes darted back and forth as Cora led him to a quiet table at the back of the diner, close to the kitchen's swinging rear door. The clanking of dishes was loud when the doors swung open.

He slid easily into his seat, leaned forward with his hands clasped together on the table. His fingers were long and thick, fingernails dirty from playing ball in the park.

"What would you like to drink or eat, Ramon?"

He peered down at the open menu she gave him, undecided as he peered at the numerous choices. A large glass of ice water was placed beside him by Edith Waller, a weekend waitress who covered lunches and dinners on Saturday and breakfasts and lunches on Sundays. "A cheeseburger would be good. I want it well done, with raw onion on top, okay? With fries and a nice big pickle," he quickly said looking at Edith.

"Make it an extra-large burger for him, Edith. Fries too." Edith nodded and hurried to the kitchen.

"It's nice of you to buy me lunch, Mrs. Gus. I appreciate it after working out. My mother tells me I'm always hungry. Too hungry."

Mrs. Gus smirked. Kids his age were always hungry, but Ramon Maldonado was big for his age, almost a young teenager. "How are you getting on in school, Ramon?"

"I do okay," he replied slowly. "And next year I'll be going to high school."

"Any plans for what you want to do?"

"Make the baseball team." He beamed. "I plan on making a name for myself. I've been playing ball since we came to New York."

"Where did your parents bring you from?"

"Guatemala. I was just a year old. They travelled with a caravan. Walking most of the way. It took a long time. An awfully long time. When they came to the Rio Grande, they had to give all their money to have someone get us across. I was told it was late at night when we crossed the border. Border cops caught us right away. After a time in some detention center, we were finally sent to live with my father's family who lived here. Me, my two sisters and mother. It's been good. My uncle helped my father find work through their church. My mother helps take care of children for other people. The coach at my mother's church got me interested in playing ball for their team. I joined their club when I was eight. We meet on weekends, practice Tuesdays and Thursday in the courtyard. Coach Carlos says I have promise. Real promise." He grinned. "And I practice myself every day. In the street, throwing against the walls, playing with a couple of my friends when they're around. This is the only life I've ever known. I like it here."

"What position do you play?"

"Coach Carlos has had me try out everything. First base, third, outfield. I can even pitch sometimes. Coach says I can become a real power hitter if I keep it up. I like that. My mother and sisters come watch me play sometimes when we have games against other clubs in our age group." The grin remained. She liked his self-assured attitude. "We always win. Well, almost always."

The food came and Ramon ate enthusiastically.

She watched him while he greedily bit into the burger and chewed. He poured ketchup over the heaping portion of French fries and eagerly began to eat them too, one by one.

Cora waited a few minutes and then casually leaned in closer, lowering her voice. "I heard that you know something about the homeless guy who got beat up the other week?" she asked matter-of-factly.

He nodded while chewing the last of the cheeseburger. "Yeah. He saw me carrying my glove one day and called me over. He asked a bunch of questions about playing ball."

"Was that all?"

Ramon shrugged. "He wanted to know about my team, where we play, what my favorite position is, favorite pro teams and which players I admire. Stuff like that."

Cora motioned for Edith to come back. "How about a piece of cake or pie for dessert?"

"Do you have chocolate cake?"

"Sure. Which kind? We have everything." His smile grew wider. Mrs. Gus looked at the waitress and nodded. "Let's give Ramon a nice slice of chocolate fudge."

Edith hid her own smile and hurried off. "Did this guy ever talk to you more? Not just baseball, but maybe other things too?"

"Baseball is his thing. He knows lots about this stuff. He said I had good muscles, good posture. He could tell. I could be a power hitter maybe, with enough practice. He knows the history of all the great players. Reggie Jackson, DiMaggio, Barry Bonds, everyone. The best pitchers too." As he talked Cora could tell that the homeless man had left quite an impression on Ramon.

"What else?" she carefully asked as Edith put the chocolate cake in front of him. The boy's eyes grew large. He started to eat, talking with his mouth full, his appetite seemingly insatiable. "We met at Forest Park a couple of times. He showed me how to stand better at the plate when I swing. I showed him my bat and he gave me tips on how to hold it better, to swing low and up, not to be so rigid."

"Sounds like he's been a real help to you. That's good. Do you know his name?"

For a moment Ramon seemed suspicious at the question. "I call him Matt. He doesn't like to give names out. I suppose I wouldn't in his place either. No one cares about him, I know, but I think he's a good guy. And I'm glad he's around."

"Do you have any idea what Matt's last name is?"

Ramon thought again. "He might have told me something or other once. I don't remember. Nothing special. But he did say lots of people once knew him back home."

"Oh? Back home?"

"Yeah. He's not from around here. One time I think he mentioned being a kid from California. But that was a long time ago. He's an old guy now."

Mrs. Gus stirred. "Have you seen him since the night he was beat up?"

Here Ramon hesitated. "Why do you ask?" It seemed he was holding back something.

"I'll be honest with you, Ramon. I have a friend who also knows him a little. She helps him out now and again, and she's worried, very worried. She also heard about what happened. Naturally, she wants to make sure he's okay. I don't mean your friend Matt any harm. In fact, if I can find out who hurt him, I'll get them to pay for what they did. So, you can be truthful with me. We're on the same side. Please Ramon, tell me what you can. Anything I can find out would be a help."

"It was really bad, Mrs. Gus. This guy hurt him a lot." Ramon looked like he was holding back tears. "He didn't deserve that. This guy deserves what he gets."

"This guy?" she asked with a hint of surprise. "Only one? Not a gang?"

"I don't know who, but it was only one guy who did it to Matt."

"How do you know?"

Ramon bit his lip, met her gaze evenly. Now he spoke slowly, in a very low voice. "Matt told me the story about that night. You know, the night it was raining so hard the other week."

She felt a lump rising in her throat, and her heartbeat quicken. "So, you've seen Matt? You know where he is?"

He gazed at her closely, deciding if he could trust her. "I do know where he was hiding himself a couple of days ago."

"Please have confidence in me, Ramon. Help me find him. I can be of assistance, get him some real help, and get him to heal properly. All of his secrets are safe with me, I promise. And you'll be doing Matt a favor, Ramon. A big one. Take me to him."

"He's really afraid, Mrs. Gus. You know? He doesn't trust people anyway. And now, after what happened, I don't know how he'll react. He may not even be in the same place. He moves around, you know. I don't always know where to find him."

"I understand, Ramon," she replied in a reassuring voice. "But he has nothing to fear from me, or any of my friends." She swallowed, then added, "Believe me, I also know what it's like to be alone and really afraid."

5

IT WAS A MURKY, WET night. Dirk used his key and quietly came into Cora's dimly lit parlor. She had been sitting sleepily on the couch waiting. At sight of him she dashed over and clutched him closely against her. He looked terrible. Fatigued, eyes bloodshot, his face appearing sunken amid the shadows. "Don't turn on the light," he said.

Cora stood slightly shaking at the sight. "I need to rest."

She watched him almost fall onto the couch. "What's happened? What's going on?"

"Don't look so worried. I'm all right," His voice was raspy. "I haven't slept for almost two days, I think. I just need to sleep, then I'll be good."

"I've been out of my mind all day and night. Calling and calling. No answer, no signal. I was almost ready to phone the ambassador's private number. Didn't you get any of my texts or calls…?"

He nodded weakly. "I'm glad you didn't. Everything that could go wrong did. I knew you were trying to reach me. There was no time. I can't explain now. Forgive me for not getting back to you, please. I just wanted to reach home as fast as possible."

He reached out his hand to her. She took it and knelt beside him. "Do you need water, food, anything?" There was a dark bruise on the side of his unshaven face, she saw.

"I have no appetite. But I am thirsty. Cold water would be good."

She hurried to bring him a glass of water. "At first I thought your flight must have been delayed. Storms, fog? After the airline told me your flight landed on time, they informed me that you weren't on the plane. I said I was from the American Embassy and to double and triple check. They said you'd made a reservation, but the airline kept insisting you were a no show. You hadn't cancelled. There were no explanations. I didn't know what to think, Dirk. I kept calling all around. Other airlines, trying to find out if you changed flights at the last minute…"

"I crossed the border by car." He said at last.

"By car?" She was puzzled. "You came back to Athens by car? There's no direct border crossing from Istanbul. Dirk, what's going on? This isn't normal. Please, just tell me." Worry mingled with frustration in her voice.

"I drove almost all night, finally managing to cross back into Greece from Bulgaria. At dawn, from the frontier. It was difficult. Soldiers were checking all cars for some reason. My Turkish contact hadn't shown, even alternate plans got screwed up, changing almost by the hour. I had to leave Turkey. Don't worry, the embassy knew about my alternative route. No need to be upset. I promise you everything is under control." He drank deeply from the offered glass. Wiping his mouth, he added, "I received some last-minute instructions regarding a Bulgarian contact. Bureaucratic nonsense. Everything threw me badly off schedule. I had to rent a car."

"And you wound up at the Bulgarian border? It makes no sense." She bit her lower lip, shifting uncomfortably. "I didn't go into work today. I couldn't go in. Not upset the way I've been. I was so frightened, Dirk. So very scared something bad had happened. Knots in my stomach all day. I made a few calls to Sandy Miller at the embassy, and she tried to help me out. Eventually I wound up speaking with your counterpart, Brian Downing. I didn't want to go up any higher. Brian told me not to worry, telling me I could take as much time as I need. But he asked me to phone him when you showed up. He practically insisted on it."

Dirk shook his head with annoyance. He held up his hand. "Don't call Brian Downing, Cora. Don't." He squeezed her wrist. "I'll explain everything to you later. Just let me get a little sleep. I need sleep."

His eyes closed and he fell asleep as soon as his finished his last words. Cora stood up and stared. She was now feeling more fearful than before. Dirk Bonneau, the man she was sure she would soon marry, was becoming more of a riddle than ever. She went into the kitchen and poured herself a glass of ouzo. She sat at her table, shaken, confused, afraid, trying to decide on what to do next. At least Dirk was unharmed, except for the bruise she had noticed. Thank God for that much.

Fragmented thoughts whirled through her mind. Be reasonable Cora, she assured herself. There will be an explanation. A good one, followed by a good long talk. His comings and goings were not only becoming more frequent, but somehow more mysterious. His reluctance to discuss anything was only making matters worse. The title of Special Assistant to the Ambassador didn't explain anything of his recent behavior. Her friends at the embassy did not seem to know anything about him, unlike many who came and went from country to country, working a few years here, a few years there. All she knew was that she was in love with this unusual American. He had promised her—No, they had promised each other, to always be open and honest. And Dirk was, or so she always thought. But lately, and especially these past several months, his assignments were becoming not only more frequent, but more unexplained.

He needed to sleep now, she understood. For as long as was necessary. When he woke, though, when he finally came back to himself, he would have to open himself up to her. If there was one thing she realized, she could not live her life indefinitely this way. Not like this. It wasn't fair. It wasn't honest. And whatever the truth was she would be prepared to face it fully without excuses.

The first light of dawn appeared on the horizon. The city of Athens would soon be awake. Dirk slept deeply all day and into the evening. When

Cora returned home from work, he was still asleep. As soon as he woke, he made a call to the ambassador's private number. A brief talk, and then he had to leave. "I'll be back in a few hours," he reassured her. "I've been summoned to a meeting with the ambassador in half an hour."

"Meeting Ambassador Mary Overstreet now?" Cora was surprised.

He kissed her and held her close. "I need to update her with added information we can't discuss by phone. Don't be angry with me. I'll be back as soon as I can." And he was on his way.

Cora was too irritated to contain her concern. She walked the streets for a time, avoiding busy sidewalks, sidestepping groups of tourists cheerily taking in all the sights Athens had to offer. Lyra had left numerous messages and texts on her phone, but she didn't want to talk to anyone now—anyone except Dirk. It was only a few months before they had announced their engagement. Dirk had proposed during a weekend trip they'd taken, and she, giddy with happiness and overflowing with feelings of love, had immediately accepted. Her family agreed they seemed a good couple together. Even her business-minded father remarked that the handsome American might yet turn out to be a worthy life partner. How had so many things changed since then? These feeling that kept growing, gnawing at her, telling her that something wasn't right. Something just wasn't right.

Later that evening Cora returned to find Dirk already home. "I'm sorry," Dirk began, just as Cora spoke, "It's been like a bad dream." They glanced at each other fleetingly, but some of the tension eased. They went out to sit on the balcony chairs.

Dirk took her hand. "I'm sorry. It wasn't supposed to be this way."

She stared out toward the star-studded sky, which outlined the shape of the panoramic mountains in deep black. Her shallow breaths were followed by a soft sigh. "Please," she said at length. "No more apologies. No more."

He acknowledged and said, "You think I don't understand how you feel. But I do. And I hate the fact that I can't explain everything to your satisfaction." Their eyes met. "The world we live in...our world. You see it for what it is. Everywhere. Hatreds, wars, terrors. Fear. Satellites and lasers, computers and phones, everything is a monitor. A spy. Everything is tracking everyone. And no nation is clean, no matter what governments say or try to justify. We're pawns. All of us. Trying to find some peace and love, a place to call home. You know how I feel about you, Cora. It isn't all like that." He was as sincere as he could be, she realized.

"I love you, too. What am I to say? That it's alright? It isn't. It can't ever be. I was so frightened for you." He put a finger to her trembling lips.

"We have each other, that's what counts."

She shook her head. "I don't want to lose you."

"You won't."

"I feel as though I already have. Slipping away, lost you to some damn useless cause. To your patriotism or whatever you want to call it. Something happened that you can't—or won't—tell me about."

"That isn't true."

"That is true, Dirk!" She shivered as she confronted him. "Your face was bruised. You were hurt. Something happened while you were gone to Istanbul or Bulgaria, or wherever the hell you really were but can't be honest with me."

"Please Cora..."

Her tears fell. "If it were someone else, another woman, even a damn wife, that I could fight to keep you, make a deal in some way or find a means to get you out. But it isn't that. It's something else, something worse." She searched for the proper English words. "Something insidious that I, or maybe anyone, can't battle. You call all this secrecy your work. A part of your career. Your duty to the embassy, to the fucking government, but I don't believe it. You see, I've spent my whole life seeing and watching how my father operates in business. So shrewd. So many friends, so much clandestine classified commercial involvement."

"Your father and family are successful businesspeople. Important and influential in the community. Their professional concerns aren't the same as being involved in official government levels."

"Don't be naïve, Dirk," she snorted. "Multinational corporations come asking favors, not only local businesses. And that doesn't count petty Greek government or foreign officials involved in one way or another. A wink here, a bribe there. No one gets hurt, do they? No one knows the full details, the dirty work involved. A 'special favor' gets a juicy contract. While another bidder, maybe a better one, suddenly gets conveniently shut out. Of course, no one knows why. A rash of rumors float. Lots of whispering gossip. Newspapers, television investigators decide to probe. Just like that," she snapped her fingers. "We get public outrage. Bigshot officials find microphones shoved in their faces. Nobody knows anything. Opposition politicians demand explanations, and official inquiries. The internet is abuzz. The circus goes on. Lies, shame, dishonor, humiliation follow. Someone must take the fall, right? It's all a sham. Behind-the-scenes part of an immoral, unethical game. Presidents and prime ministers resign, proclaiming innocence. And finally, after the broadcast outrage and public disgust, when all is said and done, the scandal soon gets pushed aside and overtaken by yet a new even bigger accusation of corruption. And at the end, when the show trials are finished, everyone makes money."

"Slow down, Cora. There are plenty of good people too."

"You think I don't believe what I'm saying?"

"I think you're really upset, and it's because of me."

"No, it's not just that. Do you think I don't realize the corrupt system we're living in? The European Union, China, Russia, even the wonderful United States. Give me some credit, Dirk. Maybe in the past I've been naïve. But I'm not a fool. I've been at the embassy long enough, and I have eyes and ears. The whole place is a den of spies and subversion. No one truly trusts anyone. We all pretend we don't recognize it. People have looked askance over my shoulder more than once. And I've been asked to do some internal observing myself, and quietly report what I've discovered. Where is the honor, the justice? Perhaps there never was. Just convenient lies."

Dirk gazed into the distance, bewildered by her unexpected eruption. It took him a long time to say anything. "I love you, Cora. That's what counts."

Her mouth opened but words were elusive. She hugged him, wondering if she truly believed everything she'd said.

"So much of our lives are intertwined," Dirk said in a soft tone, his gaze down at the floor. She realized he was seeking a better way to explain his work, his duties, in a manner where he could still withhold what he had to. Meanwhile, a small murmur at the back of her mind wondered how unlimited his duties really were.

Inside the chancery it was business as usual. A tax and tariff economic meeting had been going on for hours in the executive offices above. Numerous Greek and American citizens stood in long lines to renew visas and fill out business applications regarding export and import duties and exemptions.

Sandy Miller, Cora's direct supervisor, asked for help in gathering extra support staff for the overload. She didn't mention the frantic call Cora had made to her, nor any mention at all of Dirk Bonneau, Special Political Assistant to the Ambassador.

Cora spent hours dealing with consular officers, each requesting immediate access to copies of assorted documents. Mundane but imperative tasks, in keeping diverse businesspeople placated with batches of numerous forms and documentation.

When near the end of the day work quieted, Cora decided to stay late to explore recent files concerning Istanbul. Assorted dealings by the embassy to the consulate in Istanbul, as well as flights booked to the capital, Ankara, and return trips to Athens made by consular officials in the past several years. There were dozens. More than that, far more than she realized. Almost all the travel was designated as official business, all expenses reimbursed. Nothing unusual at all. One or two expenses, however, did catch her eye. A rapid trip to Istanbul, followed by seemingly unnecessary quick flights to Sofia, Bulgaria, before returning back to Athens again from Istanbul. That seemed to repeat itself several times. When she looked closer to determine who received reimbursement for the trips, the file was off-limits, inaccessible. Permission denied, classified as secret. With her experience and recent promotion Cora herself held a relatively high classified grade. This file, though, was higher than her grade allowed. Much higher. It was the same she saw for a second trip only a few weeks before, which appeared to coincide with one of the last-minute trips Dirk had made.

Looking back more than the past year or so she couldn't find other trips with the same odd itinerary, or anything else locking her out, other than material concerning Ambassador Underwood herself, who's own influential comings and goings were kept separately, and occasionally top secret.

She poured herself a cup of tea from the small pot on her desk and sipped. Then she sought Dirk's file, informally reading background information, education, qualifications, and the like. There was nothing she didn't already know. Born in Connecticut. Attended Syracuse University, R.O.T.C. scholarship, Reserve Officer Training, U.S. military, Army. Graduated with both business and political science degrees. Good grades. Upon graduation he went into the service. Army, remained stateside, left the service with the rank of captain. There was a notation of unspecified special training he received, no details. After that he spent a year working in New York City for a multinational financial corporation. All legitimate. Then he decided to switch careers and left New York, applying for a diplomatic position with the State Department. He effortlessly passed all their requirements. His first foreign appointment was in South America, a brief stint in Buenos Aires, followed by a couple of other minor stints in EU countries, and finally this promotion to Special Political Assistant to the Ambassador here in Athens. A nice jump for sure, but unsurprisingly Dirk was considered quality material, highly thought of based on his recommendations, and a potentially lifetime career ahead if that's what he decided.

Frequently high-profile ambassadors are personally appointed by the president, while others work their way up as diplomats through the State Department. The presidential appointees often come from all walks of life, many rewarded with ambassadorships for their political loyalty. The best career diplomats, though, are often experts in international relations, having proven themselves in representing all manner of United States interests overseas. It seemed a perfect fit for Dirk. Maybe it was too perfect a fit?

"'Night, Cora."

She looked up. Her nearby colleagues were going home for the day. "Staying late?" someone asked.

"A bit. Sandy needed me before. I'm making up for some lost time now."

A brief time later Dirk's colleague, special assistant Brian Downing stopped by her desk. He peered over her partition. "How are you feeling?" he asked quietly, as he chewed his gum. "Better, I hope."

She looked up at his broad, unshaven face. She hardly knew Brian, other than in passing, and that he and Dirk held similar titles and shared similar duties. Both were considered close confidantes of the new ambassador. Dirk never discussed much about Brian, hardy ever even mentioning him. That is until the other night when he implored her not to talk over anything with him. She had no idea why Dirk had said that, squeezing her wrist with a meaningful look in his eyes that told her to listen to him. It troubled her.

"Yes, much better," she remarked with a wide smile, offering no further information.

"You sounded really distressed when we talked. I was getting worried," he pressed.

"Foolish of me if I did. I do apologize. It was Sandy Miller who suggested I call you…"

He held up his hand with a smile of his own. "No need to explain anything. I'm glad Sandy suggested it, and that you're okay. Also, I'm glad to hear Dirk is fine as well."

He walked off, stopping to chat with a passing political appointee. They spoke for a few moments, shared a laugh, then walked off in separate directions. Cora waited a minute, sipping her tea, and then returned to the screen, this time looking up the dossier available on Brian Downing. She was a bit surprised to see how similar Dirk's background and dossiers were. Brian had also been R.O.T.C. at university, entered the military, left, and joined the State Department. What caught her eye was the mention that he too had received a bit of undefined 'special training' while serving his country. What did their 'special training' mean?

6

ST. JOSEPH'S CHURCH HAD BEEN built nearly a century before. A towering edifice on a major avenue in the borough of Queens in New York. The gothic stone structured church boasted a lofty tower between the chancel and nave, with tall, tapered stained glass windows standing along the sides. Cora looked around, impressed at the architecture and size, as well as the peaceful and welcoming feel. She walked down the cobblestone path leading to the large front entry. At the top of the steps Detective Jonah Hunter was sitting uncomfortably on the topmost step, sipping at a cup of coffee. On his lap he looked down disgustedly at the unappetizing peanut butter and jelly on plain white bread laying unwrapped on a paper bag. If Father Marcel hadn't returned his call so promptly, he might have had time to buy something good from Mrs. Gus at the Athena instead of this crap. Looking up, he saw a tall shapely woman in a raincoat coming his way and waving at him. Her hair was pulled back tightly into a ponytail. He put the sandwich back in the bag, stood up, and waved.

"You said to meet you at noon, Hunter," she said, reaching the steps.

It was mild, the beginning of spring showing itself with grass shoots growing in the church garden. The ground was still damp from a few morning showers.

"Let's walk for a few minutes before our meeting," he said as she approached. She squeezed his arm when he came down the last step.

"Thank you for getting yourself involved i have to. But I do appreciate your help mor

He looked at her with a small smile. ' mess either. At least I get paid for it. Anyw By the way, I did get to talk to one of th to the hospital. He didn't have much to did have something I found interesting. attends church locally here at St. Joseph's. His kius hau Also, he told me that our homeless victim used to come here sometimes. He recognized him. He doesn't know any specifics, but he is certain our guy showed up at the community dinners they hold a couple of times a month. The place fills up with homeless men, and a handful of neighborhood low-income families in need. This EMT and his wife volunteer and are familiar with most of the outreach events St. Joseph's organizes. He says he'd seen the victim coming to community meals on at least several occasions. Even recently." Jonah Hunter sipped his coffee. "More than that, it seems Father Marcel, the head priest, has had conversations with the guy. Don't know about what, but I when I called Father Marcel explained everything, he knew who I meant. He even knew about the beating. That's when I asked him to talk about it whenever he had time. He said today would work to squeeze us in because he's leaving tonight for a few days. So that's when I decided I'd better call you right away, Mrs. Gus."

"Do you know Father Marcel well?"

"No. I don't go to church. Ever. I don't believe in anything anymore. Do you ever come here? Are you Catholic?"

She shook her head. "I was raised Orthodox. Greek Orthodox. But I haven't been inside a church now I guess for more than twenty years." He glanced at her. "But never mind all that," she added, "tell me what you can about Father Marcel."

"He's got a good reputation, for sure. I've never heard anybody speak badly of him. And he's been involved in this parish a long time. But this

ce. The diocese considers him one of their best. Beloved
He knows lots of people, those that count and those that
ttle transpires in the neighborhood about which he hasn't
, if what he and our victim discussed wasn't done during confes-
he'll be able to fill us in."

At that moment, a slender figure emerged from the door, as if on cue.
He was very tall, wearing a white collar. "I'm ready whenever you are detective," he called at sight of Hunter and his companion strolling nearby. He
greeted them both enthusiastically at the door.

When he was introduced to Mrs. Gus the priest welcomed her like an
old friend come home. "So, you're the famous Mrs. Gus I've heard so much
about. The Athena Diner is alleged to be the best diner in all of the city,
people told me," he said with a gleam. He had a slight accent, she noticed,
possibly French or French-Canadian. His slender face and thinning hair
were offset by a pair of deeply set dark blue eyes. The eyes behind rimless
glasses penetrated with what Cora considered to be a wise and worldly air.
The good priest had been around the block.

"Please, do come inside. My excuse for an office is close."

They entered the church into the vestibule. The sanctuary was quiet,
containing the hint and ambiance of something sacred, Cora thought. It
reminded her of such places in her own distant past. Numerous pews on
each side of the main aisle only hinted at the vast size of St. Joseph's. The
stained-glass windows poured colorful light within, and the lofty ceilings
punctuated the distant altar and the sanctuary lamp suspended above it.
The overall impression conveyed was massive, yet simultaneously provided a feeling of profound intimacy. Difficult to describe, she was immediately moved.

He gestured toward the doorway that led to his office. Bookcases and
books were strewn everywhere. He lifted several piles off the chairs in front
of his wide wooden desk. A laptop and small printer sat on another pile of

books. "Can I offer you fresh coffee, or perhaps tea?" he asked, as he filled a large mug with hot black coffee from a waiting pot.

Hunter let him refill his takeout paper cup. Cora thanked him but declined.

Father Marcel slipped into his well-worn leather chair behind the desk and looked at them both with a friendly grin. It squeaked as he leaned back. "So now, how can I be helpful to you today?"

"Thank you for seeing us so quickly," Hunter said, taking a creased paper from his sport jacket pocket. It contained the EMT report of the beating, and he passed it across to Father Marcel. The priest put on his glasses and glanced at it. He winced. "Not a pretty picture, is it, detective?"

"No Father, it's as ugly as it gets. I wish I could report otherwise, but we have no leads on who might have done this. I have a hunch this beating possibly wasn't a random assault. I'm thinking this particular perpetrator had some prior knowledge of the victim."

"Because of the severity of the beating," Cora added. "This was more than a robbery of chance or some momentary anger. It sickens me to think of how severely he was hurt. The offender inflicted unnecessary damage. No reason for that. No known reason, that is."

The priest listened attentively. It wasn't the first time the police had come to him and asked for help. Especially in serious cases involving people he might have had contact with. Crime overall had certainly increased since the pandemic. That had become a fact pretty much everywhere.

This attack, though, appeared a bit different. It wasn't about robbery, seemingly not for drugs, nor a sexual assault of any kind. It had been a blatant brutal beating. Savage. Even if money were owed by the victim for booze or drugs, this level of violence was unwarranted. Excessive in cruelty, as he had heard it spoken about several times in recent days. He sat quietly. It was indeed shocking.

"So, why do this to someone?" Father Marcel said after a time.

"A theory both Mrs. Gus and I have is that it's some sort of revenge. Someone getting even. Payback, maybe. A person our victim might know, or at least have had dealings with."

At length, Father Marcel leaned back and heaved a sigh. "So, you think I'll be able to help you in some way? What would you want me to do?"

Hunter looked over at Mrs. Gus and motioning for her to talk first. "I understand that this man, our victim, has been coming to St Joseph's frequently," she began. "Please believe I want to do what I can to find and help him, as well as learn whoever did this. A friend of mine who befriended our victim is in agony over what happened. She's sick to death over it. We know he's been released from the hospital, refusing all but emergency treatment at his first opportunity. That's our top priority--locating him and doing whatever possible to get him healed and keep him safe. The thug who did this may still be lurking, biding his time. Searching in the same way we are. We need to find him first." She spoke in a soft tone but the anger underneath her demeanor was obvious.

"I understand. You make your point very well."

"Then will you assist us, Father? Please?"

He met her hopeful eyes. "I give you my word. I'll do whatever I can. But you know I haven't seen your victim since this incident. I have no idea where he might be now. Someone might be hiding him, taking care of him...or he might be alone in the shadows of some dark alley. Both are possibilities."

"What can you tell us about him?" asked Hunter, shifting in his chair. "Anything at all he said to you could prove valuable. Anything of course that isn't confidential between the two of you."

The astute priest studied his guests, taking his time, measuring them up in his mind. Detective Hunter he knew for some time and liked. He had heard of the attractive Greek woman who owned the nearby diner. Several of his friends and congregants frequented the eatery, often praising it, as well as mentioning the interesting lady who owned and operated it. It was no secret she often dealt with matters beyond those typical of a restaurant owner. Sometimes, it was alleged, she delved into serious, even potentially dangerous matters. This widow, this immigrant to America who'd made a formidable name for herself and developed such sturdy roots. The unwavering investigator who works for no fee. Now here she was, sitting a mere few feet away, unmistakably eager, smart, and ready to fight for her cause. His curiosity about Mrs. Gus increased.

"I'd say Mitch first began coming to the church more than a year ago, Mrs. Gus. Community meals for those in need."

"Mitch?" she interrupted. "I was told his name was Matt or Matthew."

He put his palms outward. "I only know him as Mitch. Or Mitchell. I never questioned it. You already know we hold regular community dinners without cost to anyone attending. A donation is gratefully accepted, naturally, but never required, or ever asked. There's a charity box at the door. Mitch began showing up maybe a bit more than a year ago, as I was saying. Noticeably quiet, he was in the beginning. He always sat by himself, grizzled, and hunched, usually at the end of a row so he could get up and leave quickly. He also caught my attention because he never seemed to be happy. I found that odd. Most men like him, destitute individuals I mean, are generally quite fortunate to be given a good hot meal, especially when there are always seconds available, and sometimes even some leftovers to take away with them. They banter among themselves; they laugh loudly and stay in good spirits when they leave. Sometimes they surprise me and interact with families that also come, especially when there are some children. Often, they like kids. Mitch never seemed to. In fact, it was my impression that he avoided them. Also, I saw there was a deep despondency about him. I watched him. He always ate his meal slowly, patiently. He had good manners, I noticed. He sat up straight, using his knife and fork. He had good posture. None of this is at all typical for men so depressed, so down and out, outcasts from society. Even more so with men who abuse drugs and alcohol. If nothing else, his manner indicated he'd had a good upbringing."

"When was it that he first approached you to talk?" Hunter asked.

"He didn't. I approached him. If I recall, the first time I tried to get to know him, I made some excuse and asked him if he minded giving me a hand moving a bunch of dirty trays back into the kitchen. God has blessed us with a pretty large operation down in our basement. Large enough to feed more than a hundred if necessary. Mitch didn't hesitate when I asked. He appeared strong and able for someone living life on the streets. Although his clothes were as shabby as any of the others, and from afar you'd never set him apart, somehow he was different." Father Marcel paused, closed his eyes for a moment in introspection. "How can I explain it? There was an air of pride about him. A quiet dignity. It was a curious thing. I wondered about him, his past, who he was or had been. And what awful things might have happened in his life…"

"Sounds like he stumbled somewhere in a big way," said Cora.

"A very big way," confirmed the priest. "I can only conjecture from bits and pieces he'd said at various times."

"Please go on," said Hunter, beginning to take notes on his phone. "Consider our talk today informal. Nothing discussed has any kind of intent or malice. I'm not here to accuse anyone of anything or try and solve some forgotten cold case."

"All right. Let me begin to tell you. The little bit Mitch talked that evening I noted a hint of an accent. Not foreign. American. Not from New York, though. Maybe somewhere out on the West Coast."

"California?"

"Perhaps." Father Marcel took a long draught of his coffee, placing his mug squarely in front of him. "I asked him a couple of harmless questions. I didn't want to be too forward, make him think I was prying. Mitch hesitated at first, but then he mentioned that he'd traveled far and wide for most of his life. All across the country. Living for a time in Arizona, then making his way north, Michigan, then remaining a while in Chicago. He mentioned Pittsburgh too, I think. Odd jobs he said. A refinery somewhere for a time, then something to do with trucking. Not long haul, just local stuff. Going from job to job, earning enough money to afford a room, food, and doubtlessly spending the rest on alcohol. I've seen so many poor souls who live that way. During another visit I mentioned that I was from Montreal. His eyes lit up at that. He told me he liked Canada, except for winter. He started to say something about 'playing there'…then stopped. 'Playing there?' I repeated. I assumed he might have been in a band of some kind. I tried to get him to tell me more about it, but he wouldn't. One other thing I can tell you, though. When he speaks, he speaks well. I got the impression he's well educated. Not at all a dropout."

"You sound like you were quite impressed," said Mrs. Gus.

"Not so much that, as to how he might have fallen so far, for so long. I'd guess he's spent decades this way. Itinerant, roaming the landscape, drifting from place to place, going everywhere and nowhere…"

"Anything make you wonder if he'd ever found himself in trouble with the law?" asked Hunter.

"Not dealing drugs or committing armed robbery if that's what you mean. I don't know if he spent time in prison. But who knows what makes people tick? When you scratch the surface, you begin to learn so many things in so many ways. It's discouraging." He frowned, countless recollections coming to mind.

Mrs. Gus edged forward. "You mean the things you hear during confession?"

He pursed his lips. "Well, Mitch wasn't a penitent. After thirty-five years wearing this collar, you hear everything. It's sad how people can change, you know. When you're young everything looks so possible, doesn't it? You'll conquer the world. I thought that. Then slowly, and sometimes not so slowly, life abruptly kicks you in the gut."

Cora flinched and felt a tightening in her stomach as he said that. For a moment she was sure the priest had noticed her discomfort, and she quickly tried to hide it. "Some people are luckier than others," she said.

"You must see quite a lot of this sort of thing yourself, Mrs. Gus., working with the public every day the way you do." He glanced out of his window, realizing he might have touched on something distressing in her life, and he didn't want to make her uncomfortable. "Of course, everyone is forgiven who honestly repents, no matter what they've done."

"Did he ever mention family," she quickly said.

"No. I did ask him about that. It seemed obvious that was a topic he didn't want to discuss. I don't know if he was ever married or has any children. Nor anything about his parents. Not even a word about sibling. He's very silent on those things. Nothing ever personal, I mean too personal for him. I offered to hear his confession many times. He did tell me he was raised Catholic. But he always refused my offers. My assistant, Father Jerome, also attempted to befriend him, but Mitch didn't take to him. I'm the only one he ever had any lengthy conversations with. To me Mitch is a gentle man. There was that one time, though. The single exception. When he got into a fight."

Hunter made a few more hasty notes. "Oh? When was that?"

"Maybe a month ago. One of the other regulars was sitting close to him and kept saying things. He was getting on Mitch's nerves I could tell, and it only became worse by the minute. The man nearby became offensive, getting under his skin. You could clearly see Mitch getting heated.

"'You were a real hotshot, weren't you?' I heard the man tell him. Mitch glared, saying nothing. His antagonist didn't pause. 'A real hotshot. But you finally got your face pushed deep into shit, huh? And everybody knew it too...' Then he laughed mockingly. Mitch had enough. He got up fast, leaned across the table and grabbed this guy by his shirt. Hard. Threatening, ready to hit him. He said something like, 'Shut up, you little bastard!' Both Father Jerome and I quickly interfered and broke it up. We don't put up with that here--ever. I took hold of Mitch's arm and separated them. Mitch didn't try to stop me. He just turned away and then walked out in a hurry.

That guy was lucky. Mitch was much bigger than this fella. Broad shouldered and still reasonably muscular. Athletic even."

"Athletic?" repeated Mrs. Gus, immediately thinking of Ramon and the baseball lessons, and how the boy had learned so much from the homeless man.

"Would Mitch fit the description of an athlete?"

"Maybe when he was younger, yes. But now he's well into middle age. Back then though, I think he might have played some sports. So many of us did and still do."

"I played first base," Hunter recalled with a reflective memory. "Hell, I wanted to be a pitcher. I had some big dreams of my own planned out back in the day."

"Ah, a ball playing detective. Interesting. You know, I was something of a fanatic. I played tennis when I was young. I was rather good too. Had coaching, almost qualified for a few minor tournaments. It was my passion. I loved it." He laughed lowly. "I guess at the end I loved the church more. That and when I learned I have asthma. So, I gave that dream up and enrolled in the Jesuit School of Theology, part of Santa Clara University. However, Mitch didn't care about that. He was really interested in hearing about my tennis days. He wanted to know everything about that time. So many questions. Where I practiced, how long I played, was I coached by a pro, and how I kept in shape for a game so physically demanding, with injuries so common. He even asked what kind of shoes I wore. That day our talk was probably the longest we ever had."

Hunter and Mrs. Gus looked at each other.

"When would you say you saw Mitch last, Father?"

"He showed up at our community dinner. Two weeks ago, yesterday. I didn't expect him to come. Not after that ugly fight."

"And did anything materialize that night? Any sort of conflict?"

Again, Father Marcel thought for a time. "No. My guess is Mitch scared that other guy for good. When he stood up to his full height and raised that fist, he looked fearsome. It even surprised me. This time was different. He didn't say anything. He nodded to me as he came in but there were no words between us. He stood in line with his tray, as usual. Volunteers served him, as always. I don't think he even said thank you or goodnight to anyone, as he always had before. There were leftovers available, but he ignored the waiting bags with food. I assumed he was still upset, maybe even reluctant to return. I wondered if that other guy knew him from somewhere and wanted to rile him. That running into him here was strictly coincidence. Who knows?"

Hunter continued with his notes while Cora shut her eyes, engrossed in contemplation. Maybe, just maybe, a few things were coming together. She needed to talk with Hunter in private.

7

"*KATHIGITIS* PETRAKIS. PROFESSOR PETRAKIS. YIANNIS Petrakis."

"That's his name. Everyone knows it. He's a firebrand. A radical of the most extreme sort, charismatic, with razor sharp intelligence. He's been on watch lists for many years, and also believed to have stealthy connections with known terrorist groups across the Middle East. There's speculation he used his contacts that led to the Al Qaeda attack in London last month. He's been watched by the Greek police, the Russians, the Israelis, and of course the Americans. Interrogated numerous times, but never once charged. Never found deliberately involved with any plot or crime. Ostensibly nonviolent, all we know is he's been intimately involved in one way or another with proxy terror groups. Not just an instigator. Reputed to be a planner, a chilling strategist. Architect yes, not a participant. He's too clever. Worse, he instills hatreds into his students while portraying himself as utilizing 'free speech'. Unapologetic, he capitalizes on their youth and vulnerabilities. He alternately has backed fanatic insurgency and revolution stretching from the Eastern Mediterranean all the way to Yemen. Promoting holy causes to fight for, and even die for."

"Professor Petrakis still teaches at the university, doesn't he? I remember not wanting anything to do with him."

"For decades, yes. His mouth has made him numerous enemies, but he remains enormously popular, especially with foreign students."

Dirk pushed the thin pale curtains aside and looked out the window. He had come to love Athens during his time here, its beauty and allure, the magic fascination of its history, but also because he saw Cora as the free-spirited embodiment of her homeland. For him, the two were captivatingly intertwined. His mind jumped from thought to thought, looking for and hoping to find a way to ease her fears, and what he knew to be her growing mistrust.

She sat nearby at the end of the couch with a book opened on her lap. For the past hour she had listened in brooding silence as he spoke. "And why now are you telling me all this?" she wondered at length.

He turned to face her. "Because I want you to know. I want you to be able to share a part of my work to ease your mind. To make you see I'm not involved with anything to do with the things causing you worry and bewilderment. To realize you really can trust in me."

"So, he's part of a file you keep, you're telling me."

"One of many files. Lots of classified stuff that really needs to be declassified. I'm not divulging any hush-hush secrets. Anyone can look up Petrakis, and lots of others like him too. You deal with similar matters yourself."

"And this trip to Bulgaria?"

"A fluke. A stupid fluke. A ridiculous mistake on someone's part either on our side or in Istanbul. Plans got tangled. Wrong contact, wrong timing. Everyone's overloaded with work, and there's no money coming here for additional staff. The ambassador has tried and tried again. The State Department keeps turning her down. As a member of the EU, Greece gets a small slice of the pie. The rest of American dollars goes to bigger fish and our people covering EU headquarters in Brussels. What goes on there boggles the mind. We're all amazed they function as well as they do. Not that Greece doesn't have issues of its own we need to deal with. That's our official priority."

He walked over to her and sat on the floor at her bare feet.

She ran her fingers through his hair. "So many other things you can't disclose. I know it, you know it."

"Please, Cora." He looked at her with a plea in his eyes.

She felt at a crossroad. Dirk was trying as hard as he could to account for the undertakings he couldn't honestly explain. Her heart told her to let this circumstance go, Dirk loved her, and if there were matters—confidential matters—that he was forbidden to divulge, why should she rebuke him? Yet the nagging feeling in her gut still troubled and wouldn't go away. She bit her lip, sighing.

"Just one question, Dirk Bonneau. What was your reason for bringing up this well-known activist professor?"

She knew she was being provocative, not wanting to fully let her doubts go. If only she could understand why he's been acting the way he has. "Please..."

"Yes, Cora." There was emotion in his husky voice. "I haven't been trying to keep secrets from you, but it's true I have tried to keep you safe from becoming vulnerable."

"Vulnerable?" she repeated with widening eyes.

"Just listen. This professor, this Petrakos guy, our intelligence regarding him has been steadily reporting that he, among several other professors, have renewed secret connections with Islamic terrorists located throughout villages in the northern mountains. The Rhodope Mountain chain that crosses Bulgaria and spills over into northern Greece."

"The area of ancient Thrace," she said knowingly.

"Yes, exactly. So-called freedom movements mostly situated in parts of Ancient Thrace. A number of Bulgaria's hydropower resources happen to be located in the western parts of the mountain range. We don't know the scope of what or who may be in danger. I can frankly tell you that the Russians have quietly been in contact with our State Department, and understandably also increasingly concerned about destabilizing this entire region. Southern Europe itself could be in danger. Russia has agents positioned in Sofia and other places to report on potentially serious occurrences amid the dense forest territories up north. These present threatening events for a number of countries. What if other nearby nations are playing roles in helping to supply these terrorists? Opening a new terrorist front across Southern Europe? Albania, or Turkey, with possible new mischief from Iran. Greece could find itself caught right in the middle." He emphasized the final sentence.

"There are hydroelectric plants along the Greek side of the Bulgarian border." Cora had visited the rural north and spoke with genuine concern.

"It's potentially a vast collection of targets. But nothing has been confirmed. Everything is speculation. We're keeping a low key but close monitor."

"So that explains why you were in Bulgaria."

'Sort of. My mission really had been a contact in Istanbul—but something unexpected happened. Something I can't discuss. It made my work more difficult. Leave it at that."

Cora heaved a sigh of relief. Dirk was being truthful. At last. Not explaining everything, she was sure, but at least giving a broad idea of events being kept concealed. "So, with all this facing us, what's next?"

"All we can do is observe and stay on guard."

"And your part?"

"I take orders from the ambassador. My role remains strictly diplomatic."

"Look me in the eye and promise me that."

He met her gaze evenly, squeezing her hand. "I promise."

8

"YOU CALLED FOR A CAB, Mrs. Gus?"

Standing beside the cashier, she glanced up from notes she'd hastily scribbled, tossed her notebooks into her stitched leather shoulder bag. "Yeah. Thanks, Eddie. I gotta take care of some serious business. Lock up tight, okay? I'm not sure when I'll be finished."

Eddie gave a thumbs up. She hurried down the steps.

Outside the diner the taxi stood waiting under a faint half-moon. "Where to, Mrs. Gus?" The familiar driver asked as she got in the back door.

"Hey, Pauly. Drive straight down Jamaica Avenue. I'm only going about a mile. I'll let you know where to stop."

"Sure thing, Mrs. Gus."

The El train above the avenue squealed into the station as the car took off. Rush hour was over, so the trip was fast. As they reached a major intersection of retailers, grocery stores, and several Hispanic and Asian restaurants, she told the driver to pull over. She tipped him well and got out. Daylight had disappeared and bright neon lighting greeted everywhere along the active street. The address she was looking for was right across the heavily trafficked avenue. Crowds gathered at the lights and crosswalks. Buses on both sides halted to a stop.

"Over here, Mrs. Gus!" Beside a nearby lamppost across the way Ramon Maldonado was standing, waiting as agreed. He was wearing his usual navy blue and white baseball cap, and team jacket. Colors of the Yankees. She greeted the youth cheerfully. "Hey, Ramon. Which way from here?"

"Close. Near my middle school." He indicated the way. They walked down a darkening street. The weather was warmer than usual, bringing small groups of people out from the older single family homes rubbing shoulders with rows of five and six story brick apartment buildings. They were mostly young, gathering by lit entrances, alongside cars, or standing near the corners, speaking a smattering of different languages. She over-heard a plethora of voices speaking Spanish, Russian, Korean, Chinese. Several cars stood double parked on either side. Street parking in this neighborhood, like most in New York's urban jungle, was difficult at best.

"My janitor's name is Javier," Ramon said. "He lives just down this block. He promised he'll tell you about helping the homeless man, just days after he came from the hospital. Javier didn't know his name either, or ask for one, and I didn't tell him anything. He doesn't even know I call him Matt."

Mitch was obviously using different names, keeping his identity well hidden. Mitch or Matt, or something else didn't matter. He was hiding his identity. Hunter said he'd pull as many strings as possible to get the hospi-tal to release whatever personal information they guarded in their initial report. With a bit of luck, they might possibly find a social security num-ber, or have a copy of an expired driver's license. Maybe a report of any Covid-19, or later variant shots. Any piece of information was valuable at this point.

Ramon opened a heavy wooden door into a small walkup building.

"This way," he said.

The hallway was dim and sterile. Walls painted a drab green badly in need of a fresh coat. It was an old worn building, in need of a great deal of repair. As they walked, she could hear a television playing loudly behind a ground floor apartment door.

"He lives in the basement apartment," Ramon said, opening another, heavier door. They went down the shabby, cracked cement steps. Modest pools of water stood scattered near floor-to-ceiling pipes. Glancing, she saw several with trickling leaks looking like tears dripping into one corner. Above, the ceiling was blistered with damp, fetid dirty water.

An apartment door opened on the left. A young man with a short black beard appeared. He was holding a sleeping infant wrapped in a colorful blanket. The child had an old-fashioned rubber pacifier in his mouth. He gestured for his expected guests to enter. "Please," he said. Cora wiped her shoes on the doormat.

"Javier, this is my friend, Mrs. Gus," Ramon quickly told him.

From the end of the modest room a small woman stood peeking and looked at their guest with a wholesome smile.

"This is my wife, Elvita."

"So nice to meet you both," Cora said in a pleasant voice.

"And this is my son, Javier," the father said proudly. "He was born the day after Christmas. Please sit and make yourself comfortable." He pointed to a well-worn armchair. Elvita took the baby and sat next to her husband on the floral couch. A small crucifix hung on the wall above. Ramon stood rigidly, if nervously, beside Mrs. Gus. She knew he was hoping he did the right thing by bringing her here.

Turning down an offer for coffee or soft drink Cora got to the point of her visit. She spoke her English slowly, careful to make sure Javier understood. "I don't mean to bother you, either of you, but Ramon spoke with me a few days ago, telling how kind you both were to the homeless man that was badly beaten last week." Javier shot a fast glance to the boy and looked back to his guest. Cora held up a palm before Javier said anything.

"Please believe that Ramon did the right thing. The proper thing. I gave my word to him—as I do to you—that you can believe and trust me. I only want to offer help to this man. What happened wasn't just a fight in the streets, but a serious crime. When the police locate the one who beat him, he'll pay for it. But that isn't my concern now. I'm not a cop, I don't have any role with the police in this incident. If you can assist me in any way, I'll do everything I can to help the homeless man get good treatment. You have my promise."

Javier listened and passed the infant to his wife. She lowered her eyes, caring for the sleeping infant, rocking slowly, lovingly.

Ramon quickly uttered something in Spanish and Javier nodded. Mrs. Gus wasn't fluent at all in the language, but she did understand the Spanish word *confianza*, meaning trust.

"It was a week ago," Javier said with a heavy accent, searching for the right words. He decided to speak in Spanish and let Ramon translate. "The man you're asking for I found hiding in the alley, between large trash bags ready to be hauled away in the morning by the sanitation truck. I recognized him because of his baseball cap and old coat. Hat pulled down over bandages on his face. He was sitting against the brick wall. He was asleep, but as I came close, he woke up."

"Did he know who you were?"

Javier nodded. Again, Ramon translated. "This man slept in this alley before. Months ago, he asked me if I would let him stay here at night, and not call the cops. He promised he wouldn't stay every night or cause trouble. He would go away when the sun came up. I told him it was okay if he was careful. My wife brought him a blanket and pillow that he hid behind the dumpster where he slept. She found for him a small mattress, too. I saw him resting on it sometimes. And sometimes Elvita gave him coffee or soup, sometimes sandwiches…"

"You were very kind."

"I think he is a very unhappy man. I smell the strong drink on his breath always. I look into his eyes. They are eyes of heartache. But I knew he was kind to Ramon and some of the other boys. Especially with his baseball ability."

"Ramon told me about teaching him. Please tell me what happened after he was beaten up. What then?"

The small woman looked up and spoke to her husband rapidly. Javier listened and took a sip from a can of soda. "He showed up in the afternoon," Ramon continued translating. "I was sweeping in the hallway. Poor man was limping. His face was beaten. One eye was swollen and closed. It was bandaged at the hospital. Ribs were also broken, he said. He asked, please could he stay here for a few days. To rest. The weather was getting warmer, and…" Javier choked up for a moment. Cora watched as he fought tears from forming. Elvita again spoke rapidly, adding more to the story. Again, Cora understood only one word. *Verdad*, truth.

"I told Elvita, and we brought him here to our home. She cooked him soup, changed the dirty bandages. She washed him too, with sponges. We wanted to take him to our doctor, but he refused. There is a cot in the small room behind your chair, and he slept there most of the time. There is also a small window. It faces the ally, but there is daylight, and he would look out like a child and watch the light. We fed him more, helped him stand and to walk better. But he only walked here inside our apartment. He asked us about Ramon. So, I found Ramon and brought him here to see his friend. They talked. Then the next day he left without saying why. We told him he could stay longer, but he said no. We gave him a few clothes, and a bag with some food and drink. And I offered some money, but he wouldn't take it. He said he did have another place he could go. We asked where but he didn't say. I think he was afraid to tell us anything. He thanked us many times for being good to him. Then he left. We have not seen him anymore."

"Maybe he will go back to his real home," added Ramon.

"Home?" repeated Cora. "Where?"

The boy shrugged, but Javier said in his halting English, "He talked about California sometimes. I think maybe he grew up there. He said how cold it was here in New York at this time of year, but back at his old home in California it was so warm."

"And I already told you the way he loves to talk about baseball," added Ramon eagerly. "And sometimes tennis too. Didn't he tell you that at one time he played tennis for money?"

"*Si*," said Elvita, without need for translation. "He was watching tennis on television. One day there was a special tournament..." Javier looked sharply at his wife. She took notice and suddenly stopped speaking. There was a brief moment of awkward hushed silence.

They were protecting him, Cora had no doubt. As was Ramon. Giving her some information but omitting other details.

Cora made a mental note but said nothing about it. "Please can you tell me his name? I know he uses different ones. And I understand that he doesn't want anyone to learn about him."

"We used no names. We told him goodbye and good luck. I called him *amigo*, my friend. He called me the same."

"You are good people." Cora thanked them for their assistance, offering a little cash for the baby, but they politely refused.

9

CORA GREW UNEASY. HER LEGS felt unsteady. She used the remote control to turn up the television volume.

"*...It appears there may have been more than one explosion. The blast was huge and deafening. We don't yet know the number of visitors and tourists in the vicinity of the blast, only that there were many. Several fires are still blazing. Police and army helicopters are currently hovering above the Acropolis...*"

The phone rang. It was her sister Lyra. "Cora, have you heard the news?"

"I'm watching the television right now," she said anxiously. "Hold on. They're telling some more."

"*Of course, the Acropolis Museum and its monuments represent universal symbols of Greek spirit and antiquity. It's not yet known whether what's happened is some sort of horrible accident or an act of terror. As of now, neither the police nor the Government are providing any comments.*"

The news anchor looked on in horror as a live feed from the scene appeared to viewers. Pockets of dynamic orange flames peppered the flat landscape atop the rocky hill. Billows of rapidly circulating bleak smoke rose up to the night sky. Silhouettes of dozens of first responders could visibly be seen tightly clutching huge hoses, desperately pumping water to extinguish remaining blazes. The responders rushed to different areas, while flashing emergency lights flared overhead. Above the wail of sirens, Cora could detect distant cries of injured victims as well as loud commands being issued to the squads of additional support; policemen, medical personnel, and firefighters arriving to reinforce and secure the location.

"*We are hearing unconfirmed reports of at least three dead from our sources, likely Americans, but not yet confirmed by authorities...*"

"Dirk is calling on the other line, Lyra. I'll phone you back." She changed phone lines with bated breath.

"Don't leave the apartment for any reason, Cora," she heard Dirk's dark intonation say. "Please. We don't know yet if there are more detonations coming at the Acropolis, or wherever else in the city. Nowhere across Athens is considered safe right now. I'm asking you to stay home for a while, okay?"

"What's going on? Please, Dirk. Tell me whatever you can."

"People from our embassy are already on site. There was a private party for special guests tonight. These sinister explosions were probably meant for them. We know these guests were sightseeing the Acropolis Museum. Maybe a few Brits also. Not sure yet. A couple of embassy people were escorts, as well as several Greek guides. British embassy reps are also heading for the scene. I'll be home ASAP, but don't expect me until extremely late. They have me involved in helping coordinate things here. We'll have a crew of specialist investigators heading to the site in short order. It's a mess."

"So, no news on what caused the blasts?"

"We're fairly sure it was a bomb or multiple bombs. Probably exploding outside the entrance to one or several of the museums. Unconfirmed so far. Apparently, a warning phone call was made to the Greek Ministry of Culture, with threats of some kind. It's unclear who or why, or what they wanted. The entire district surrounding the Acropolis is being cordoned off as we speak. Traffic is blocked, backed up for miles. Everyone is being stopped and checked for ID. A few potential suspects have been pulled aside for questioning. There's speculation that the Greek government has dispatched emergency orders for military assistance in search and rescue. Everything's in flux and extremely dangerous. Just stay put. Okay?"

"Okay. Don't worry. I'll be at home. Call again when you can."

With a pant she put down the phone and stared back at the television screen. She kicked off her shoes and crossed her legs on the couch. The news kept repeating and she sat waiting for updates. After a while of listening to talking heads, she found herself drifting off. She woke with a start. New bulletins reported that representatives from the American Embassy were on the scene alongside the Hellenic Police Anti-Terrorist units. She stared, sure she caught a glimpse of Brian Downing in the background, no doubt serving in official capacity, speaking with and directing various officials gathered behind hastily constructed police barriers.

The front door opened, and Dirk quietly came in. He was expecting Cora to be fast asleep. It was almost four in the morning. She ran over and hugged him. "I'm frightened," she said in a rasping tone.

"It's under control, Cora. Believe me, everything's going to be all right. Things are finally getting organized." With his arm around her he led her toward the bedroom. "Just stay close tonight. Stay close."

* * * * * * * * * * *

CORA HELD UP HER ID card. A vigorous combat-attired Hellas Anti-Terrorist officer examined it carefully, fiercely observing her face and comparing the photo on the documentation. Satisfied after a brief check, he signaled permission for her to enter embassy quarters. Stern-faced American marines standing guard double checked her credentials and allowed her through. There was a flurry of excited activity in the embassy lobby. She saw Brian Downing. "Can you give me any news?" she asked breathlessly.

"You'd better get inside quickly. A statement is being readied for the ambassador to read to the press," Brian told her. Moments later the ambassador appeared, heavily escorted by a handful of plainclothes security walking towards an outside makeshift podium.

A solid line of Greek police officers and a contingent of American marines conspicuously guarded Queen Sophia's Avenue surrounding the embassy. Behind police barriers stood a huddle of television cameras and reporters from EU countries and the United States. Journalists were shouting questions atop one another at the ambassador and her aides while the Americans hastily prepared for the conference. A slew of microphones pointed directly at the lectern. Media reporters pushed themselves closer until the small lectern was tightly enveloped. The clamor of questions ceased as Ambassador Mary Overstreet took the podium.

Her demeanor was severe and harsh in the thin early morning light. She glanced quickly over several pages of notes and newly scrawled information. Two dour high ranking Greek police officials flanked her. Standing among a clique of inner-circle advisors behind the ambassador was Dirk. Cora stood attentive near the entrance.

One of the political deputies introduced himself, and promptly turned the microphone over to the ambassador.

"Yesterday evening a group of invited American guests were escorted for a private tour of the Acropolis here in Athens," she began. "Events are moving fast, and I can only provide you with the latest updates I've been given." As an assortment of loud questions rose again the ambassador glanced from side to side and raised her hand demanding quiet. The crowd of reporters settled down.

"At this point we believe two powerful bombs exploded outside the gates near the theater of Herodes Atticus, as well as the Acropolis Museum. As of now we are aware of three people killed, two men, one woman. I have no names to give yet. Six injured are currently being evaluated at two Athens hospitals. Four of the six are currently believed in critical condition. The United States, based on initial intelligence provided by Greek authorities, believes this to have been a deliberate calculated act of terrorism. As to who or which group may be responsible, we have no information yet. And no one, to my knowledge, has so far claimed or taken responsibility for this barbarous act. However, be assured that the American government will spare no effort in assessing who was responsible, tracking them down no matter how long it takes, and bringing all perpetrators to justice."

She paused and a boisterous torrent of questions erupted both in English and Greek. It was difficult to understand anything above the uproar. Mary Overstreet thanked everyone and quietly stepped aside to permit one of the Greek officials to respond to the press.

"Is that really everything we know? said Cora, shocked, and visibly upset.

"Everything is still confusing, and too early to decipher," answered Brian. "Had the bombs already been placed, waiting to be set off by a timer or cell phone? Was someone hiding in waiting to throw them? We don't have evidence of a suicide bomber. Were the fanatics responsible local idealogues, or foreign agents? Religious zealots, psychopaths, protestors twisted by some ideology? Or could it have been a loner eager to make a name for himself? There's so much to examine. And lord knows there are no shortages of active terrorist groups out there, lurking and eager to kill more Americans."

Greece had usually served as a place of transit for terrorist groups, Cora knew. It provided a central location in Southern Europe to which they travelled, then left for bigger destinations. It made this callous act even more shocking. Cities across Europe, especially London, Paris and Brussels were on red alert.

During the following days it seemed to Cora the entire world had changed. Colleagues at work spoke little, kept their heads down, and the atmosphere remained grim and somber. A new clandestine security team arrived from the State Department overnight, as well as an FBI anti-terrorist unit led by a team leader called Jamie Van Nostrand. Cora was familiar with that name. Van Nostrand had been something of a frequent visitor to the embassy these past several years, and Cora also knew he maintained a working relationship with Dirk. All embassy files were now being redacted, and reclassified into new confidential, secret, and top-secret categories. All computers were being scanned and improved with the latest versions of software and operating systems installed, assessed for hacking, then enhanced with the newest security measures available. Controlling and monitoring all visitors became a new crucial component, and intrusion detection systems were improved. For all intents and purposes the embassy had turned into Fortress America, as many of the staff now referred to it. For now, a state of emergency was kept in place.

All of Athens' inhabitants found themselves on edge. News reports of the Hellenic Anti-Terrorist Police stepped up combing the city and surrounding areas. Nothing at this heightened level had ever happened before. Employees of all grade levels working at the embassy, American as well as Greek, were being advised not to discuss any work matters outside, not even with family. Senior staff no longer stopped to chat with lower level personal. Cora had never felt so awkward and unnerved. For several nights Dirk remained at work overnight, along with Brian Downing, Ambassador Underwood, and a select number of others. The rumor was that Jamie Van Nostrand and several of his people were now running the show. Cora found that hard to believe, but the embassy environment was certainly altered. All night meetings became routine. Daylong strategy sessions became the norm for the upper echelons. When Dirk at last did come home, he was constantly exhausted. Cora did her best to try to keep things cheerful, feed him dinner, serve several glasses of wine, although often he wasn't hungry and just wanted to sleep. When he did talk, he purposely kept their conversations light, with no discussion of what had transpired, nor any added information regarding what was being discussed or planned in wake of these horrific killings.

Cora found herself growing more uneasy. She left on the television, constantly tuned to a twenty-four-hour international all-news station. She became irritated at repetitions of the same old news, impatient to finally hear any up-to-the-minute news. Something, anything, that might facilitate solving the mystery behind the bombings. Genuine new reports, though, were scarce. Constant interviews with more so-called experts conjecturing, speculating and building ever more fantastic theories. They appeared to know little more than anyone else, amid all the talk of the myriads of groups who might be responsible.

Because of the gag order requested by the embassy, she found herself guarded in what she could say, unable to speak openly even with Lyra or her mother. Before opening her mouth, she had to sift through her words for classified information. And more and more material was being upgraded daily. Self-censoring was tedious, so she often didn't bother to speak. It became a difficult and draining way to live.

After a week Dirk finally returned home on time. She heard the key in the door and ran from the kitchen. He looked haggard and limp. Lips dried and chapped; his eyes lacking luster. She hugged him close, and they kissed deeply.

"I don't mean to scare you," he uttered with a hoarse voice.

"I've been pretty uptight all week." She tried to help him feel relaxed and at home. "Come and sit with me. I've made us salads. Are you feeling hungry now?"

"I will be soon. But a drink would be good." He made his way to the couch, yanked off his shoes, and leaned far back into the thick pillows. She handed him a glass of wine, which he drank eagerly. "Nonstop meetings and long-distance calls," was all he said.

"Sounds like a routine day now."

"Things should get better soon. We're making some progress, I think."

"Good to hear." Cora knew it was futile to try to get him to tell her things he couldn't. "You don't have to move. We can eat here on the sofa. I'll bring trays. Then let's go to bed early."

"Eating from trays in front of the T.V. Sure. Okay. Reminds me of when I was a kid."

She tousled his hair. "You still are like a kid."

He pulled her close next to him. "You've changed my life, you know that."

"You've changed mine, too."

"You know, I used to wonder who the woman would be that I might spend the rest of my life with. I never imagined I'd find her in Greece."

"And found her at work, too. How easy for you." The humor broke any remaining tension.

"My parents didn't have a good marriage," he said thoughtfully, sipping at his chardonnay. "They'd fight all the time; I've told you that. But I'm not sure I've ever told you how at night me and my older brother Kenny, sharing a room, would wake and hear their shouting. I would cry a lot. At school Kenny would tease me but at home he protected me when I was scared. Their fights were constant, but sometimes they got really bad. And to me it all seemed over nothing. So stupid. They could have talked, hashed things out. Compromised, maybe. But they didn't know how. They were so filled with anger, viewing things from their own narrow minds. My dad always said he was going to leave. My mom told him to get out any time he wanted. They were so different, and never tried to understand each other. It was sad. Such an awful way to spend a life…"

"We're not like that."

"No, we're not. Thank God for that."

"Perhaps you being around them may have given you the spark to join the foreign service. To become a diplomat. Bringing people together, give and take, to try and sit them down and find ways to make life better for everyone."

He grinned. "You should have been a shrink."

"A shrink?"

"A psychologist. A therapist."

She laughed again. "Of course, I know what it means. I majored in English. I used to read trashy American novels all the time during my breaks."

He frowned. "Over the next few days maybe you can find another novel to keep you busy." She stared at him. "I only got word today, Cora. I have to leave for a couple of days. Not for long. I'll be back."

She pulled away. "Now? With Athens in crisis, with America searching for terrorists, they have to send you away again? Why?"

"A direct order. I'll be back as soon as I can."

"And where to this time?" She trembled as she spoke, her anger rising at the absurdity of it. If ever he was needed here that time was now.

He sighed. "Up north. Near the border."

"Bulgaria again? Of course." He reached out to her, and she pulled away.

"We're not like my parents, remember?"

Tears welled up unexpectedly from her eyes. She unsuccessfully tried to hide them. "What's the use…"

"Please, Cora. Let's not fight. I love you. I'll always love you."

Her anger quickly subsided, and she squeezed his hand. "I love you, too."

They ate quietly, without speaking much. They went to bed early and made love with urgency and passion. When Cora awoke in the morning Dirk had quietly left. On a napkin on the kitchen counter, he had written in big, bold lettering, 'You are my life'.

10

"AGENTS OF THE HELLENIC ANTI-TERRORIST Police have made several arrests here in Athens regarding the killing of three Americans and the wounding of six others. The suspects are being held incommunicado under the National Emergency Act."

Cora looked up from her computer. "Any firm news on who's been arrested?"

"We think it's a couple of teachers from the university. Several professors. They're being questioned for collaboration, we think. Also a few radical students have been taken in."

"Was one of them Yiannis Petrakis? That purveyor of hate?"

"Very likely," said her supervisor, Sally Miller, as she sauntered off down the hallway. "Him and his friends are prime suspects." Her words trailed off.

Dirk had phoned briefly from Istanbul. All was well, he said, and he expected to be back in Athens within 72 hours. She told him of the arrests; he had already heard it from someone at the embassy. It was good hearing his voice, even though she wished he'd be home tomorrow. More than anything now, she wanted to feel his arms around her at night. Hear his reassuring voice.

Hectic was the best word to describe the following days at the embassy. She was instructed to translate a number of Russian documents into Greek as well English, and to assist a low-level Russian Embassy staffer who needed to receive several quickly approved visas, requiring approval from the State Department. The Russian was aggravated, not having his needs fulfilled quickly enough, and as she tried to deal with his irate embassy new instructions were coming in for trade negotiation documents to be speedily translated into legal English. Cora was good at her work and managed to deal with it all, although it left her exhausted and edgy.

The next evening, she was happy when Lyra invited her to come over for supper. The weather was getting warmer, the days longer. Flowers were in bloom, grass was thick, trees sprouted with leaves of all colors. Athens was alive again. Calm was restored, events of the past several weeks seem to have happened a long time ago. Markets filled with shoppers, streets with strolling lovers. It was good to see. Even the mood at the embassy had improved. She even noticed Ambassador Underwood holding a cheerful luncheon for special visitors newly arrived from New York, while Jamie Van Nostrand and his FBI crew remained low key and quietly diligent going about their work.

Lyra was in a good mood when she came in. The two of them would be dining alone tonight, her husband and daughter away at a Bolshoi Ballet performance for which their father had managed to acquire tickets.

They ate out on the terrace, enjoyed the ouzo and the wonderful views. The breeze was delightful. A small radio tucked in the corner played a variety of Greek folk music.

They chatted for a long while, mostly Lyra talking about her husband and his work, and what was new among some of their relatives. They discussed the possibility of the two of them taking a short vacation during summer, maybe a fling to Cyprus. There was little mention of the embassy, current news or politics. Their father was on his way back from a business trip to Paris, where he and a partner were looking for a distributor of goods recently acquired from Vietnam. It was a pleasant evening, and Cora found herself feeling more at ease. As the hour grew late they shared one more glass of ouzo to cap the night off.

When she left her sister's spacious apartment, she walked down the broad stone staircase and came out into the street while the sun was fading. She decided to walk home, making a point of going along quiet side streets. The smell of fresh cooking lingered in the air. *Tefliko*, lamb, garlic, *keftethes*, meatballs, wafted past her nostrils. Families talking and laughing on their balconies dotted both sides of the street. Normal life for Athenians. Tasty food, good wine, good company.

Sally Miller had sent her a text asking if she could get to work an hour early tomorrow to help with the backlog that never seemed to go away. Of course, she would.

The sun had set behind romantic Mount Lycabettus by the time she reached her building. A neighbor greeted her as she came in and he went out. She smiled and said hello. The ouzo still left her with a buzz, and when she entered her flat she opened the windows wide in the front room, facing the street.

There was a loud noise in the distance. Not too far. Her heart raced as she hurried onto her terrace. She braced her hands against the stones of the terrace wall. A police car's siren blared. Then things quieted. No signs of commotion. A car crash somewhere? She drew a deep breath and filled her lungs, letting the air out slowly. Repeated a second and third time. Her nerves were frayed. She needed to compose herself. Recent events still took too much of a toll.

This too will pass, she thought. This too will pass.

She drew a bath and sank deep into warm water, gently washing with fragrant soap. Dirk was scheduled to return home tomorrow and she prayed not to get a phone call telling her he was delayed again somewhere. She washed her hair and let it dry naturally, falling slightly over her shoulders. When she was done, she drank a glass of cold water, set her clock an hour earlier to keep her promise to Sally Miller, and went to sleep.

The next morning the embassy was humming as usual. A line of travelers stood impatiently applying for visas, visitors with passes made their way down the halls past the entry with some confusion. Security politely stopped everyone, checked their passes and pointed in the right direction. The elevators opened and closed, admitting and discharging passengers. Staff from higher floors came down to greet guests with handshakes and hearty laughs. All seemed right with the world again.

A few minutes before lunch Cora received a call from the executive secretary to Ambassador Mary Underwood requesting that she come upstairs to the ambassador's private suite. Most likely it was some special assignment that needed to be done by the end of the day. Cora turned off her computer and went up to the spacious offices. When she stepped out of the elevator she saw a small group of people gathered in one of the glass suites at the end of the hall. The door opened and someone indicated for her to come in. Cora walked over casually, a professional smile on her face. "Good morning," she said, glancing around. Brian Downing was there, standing behind another senior official. All the faces were familiar, but she didn't know all their names. However, she did note that Jamie Van Nostrand was there. That seemed odd.

"Take a seat, please, Cora," said Mary Overstreet, pointing to a comfortable couch beside the wide windows. This was the first time she had been in this private meeting room.

Someone placed a pitcher of water and several glasses on the small table at the couches' edge.

It was Brian who spoke. "Cora, I have…" he corrected himself. "Cora, we have some unwelcome news we have to tell you."

She stared at him. Hints of a smile vanished. Blood drained.

"There's been a terrible event. Horrible. Dirk--"

"Is he alive?"

Total silence. Mary Overstreet sat beside her and took her hand. "A terrible, terrible, tragedy. I can't believe it myself. I'm in shock. We're all in shock. I know how close he was to you. I know—" The Ambassador broke into tears. "He was one of our best, Cora. Just know that. One of our best."

"Please tell me what this is about," Cora implored.

Jamie Van Nostrand gestured to Ambassador Overstreet, pointing to his watch.

She shook her head. "It'll wait. She deserves to know. She looked evenly into Cora's eyes. "He's gone, Cora. Dirk died in the service of his country."

Cora sat frozen, visibly paled. She felt her stomach tighten, legs begin to shake. "He's supposed to be home today..."

"We all knew how close you two were," Mary Overstreet added with conviction. "You were everything to him. I think you know that."

Brian Downing spoke up, also ignoring an annoyed Van Nostrand. "Dirk would want you to know what the ambassador's saying is true. From the first time he saw you. He knew you were the one. He told me that before he ever asked you out."

Was this real? It must be a dream, it had to be a dream. It couldn't be real. It couldn't. Brian was saying something more, but it wasn't penetrating. "Cora? Cora?"

Now it was the ambassador speaking. "We can have someone take you home. I want you to take as much time as you need. Understand? As much time—"

"When will his body be brought back to Athens? I want to see him. And funeral arrangements, when will he be buried? My family has large burying grounds."

Mary Overstreet and Brian Downing looked at each other. "Cora, he won't be brought back to Athens. Right now, he's being held by the forensic team, and then they'll fly home to Dover Air Force Base. His family lives near Chicago. His parents have already requested he be buried there."

"You have enough to deal with," Brian said quickly. "Anything, any way we can help. Shall we contact your family for you? Would you like one of our female staff to stay with you for a while?"

"We'll get you as much information about what happened when we can. We don't have details yet. You won't be kept in the dark." The ambassador waited to hear Cora's wishes.

"I'll...I'll go home." She spoke without emotion. A look of melancholy etched into her pale, delicate features. "Dirk forgot to take his electric razor. He always takes it..."

"She's in shock," Mary Overstreet whispered, her arm now tightly around Cora. Those around her agreed. "Be careful not to give her any details," said Jamie Van Nostrand, cautioning everyone in the room. "Until we get information otherwise, all of it is classified, okay? She doesn't get any more special intelligence."

"We'll tell her what we feel she deserves to know," the ambassador snapped back. "Fuck your protocol. The FBI doesn't tell me my job. Not now, not ever. I make all the decisions here until they remove me. Understood?"

Van Nostrand frowned but backed off. Gently, several staff helped Cora to stand. An embassy car was called and assigned to drive her home.

Reflexively, Cora unlocked the door to her flat.

"You're certain you don't want me to remain here with you for a while?" asked the driver in a respectful voice.

"No. You go. Please."

She tossed her purse onto the dining table and surveyed her parlor. Things appeared to be in order, exactly as she left it. The paperback Dirk had been reading was opened, face down on the table in front of his chair. The kitchen drainer held her favorite mug, and the big one adorned with the stars and stripes. Dirk's favorite. Walking to the closet she found all his clothes and shoes neatly lined up in rows. His walking sneakers. Sweaters, he liked sweaters, and a couple of stylish sports jackets.

Unconsciously she went into the bedroom. The pillows were the way they had been this morning. The one on his side still retained something of a dent from his head, barely four days before.

A spontaneous wave of grief washed over her. She lost the last of her control and fell sobbing onto the bed. Again, she prayed that this was a dream. She would wake soon. Dress for work. He would phone her and then look at the time and hurry off because he had his plane to catch, and he was again running late…

Tears flowed freely, her dark hair disheveled in front of her red eyes. She hugged Dirk's pillow as tightly as she could, trying to somehow absorb his scent. One last time, one last time. But this was the end of his future, and the end of her own. When there were no tears left, she pushed his damp pillow to the side. She stood up, unsteadily at first, feeling unable to spend another moment in this place. The warmth had vanished. Now it felt cold, sterile. An urn, she likened it to. An urn that contained the ashes of her life.

She stuffed a batch of tissues into her pocket, grabbed a sweater, and left. Into the street, with the always aromas of dinner being cooked for the many families in the area. Children laughing. Babies crying. How much she envied them now. She would gladly trade places with any one of them. She began to walk. Mindlessly, the streetlamps casting long shadows. Dogs barked from alleyways. A few cats scattered under parked cars as she passed.

Oblivious to everything, she walked for hours, aimlessly crisscrossing streets she had strolled with Dirk, and places she had never seen before. She found herself getting ever closer to the water, towards the harbor and the docks of Piraeus. A part of her mind told her to end this feeling of help-lessness, this awful misery. An urge rose and said to drown herself deep into the dark, dirty, oily seawater below.

She smiled involuntarily at the sudden sweet thought of oblivion. No more sorrows, no pain, no sad memories to haunt her. *Go on! Do it!* came the insistent voice. Why not? Who would care? Mama would. Papa. Lyra too. Others of the family. But what did they matter? Their lives were fulfilled. They had their partners, their livelihoods, their places in the world.

Still, she kept on putting one foot in front of the other. All sounds of her surroundings were dimmed by this raucous cacophony of pain in her head, running up and down her body. She ached. God, how she ached. The rhythm of her shoes tapped endlessly until she was exhausted. Her mouth was dry as a desert, her throat raw. She knew her feet were blistered and possibly starting to bleed.

And Dirk Bonneau was still dead. She wiped stale sweat and dried tears off her face and bought a soft drink from a vendor on the next corner.

She was a Drakos, she told herself. The ancestral Drakos family wasn't one to give up or give in to trouble, she knew. This she had been taught since childhood. Her forebears were fighters. Fighters against all enemies against all odds. They had fought against the Nazis, and many died for the freedom for Greece. Before then it had been the Ottomans and the Turks. Also, during the twentieth century it was a fight within against the terrible fascist military junta that had taken over this land during the 1960's and '70's.

She at once found herself reliving today. All of it. Ambassador Overstreet's explanation of Dirk's death gave her no details, despite showing concern and anguish. There were no explanations, no location, no time, no reason, no killer. True, facts were still being collected, but come to think of it, she'd be told nothing of substance. She hadn't even been told if his death was caused by accident, or was it murder? It didn't make sense. Dirk was dead, they said. We're all sorry. We feel for you. We're aware of the pain you're going through. We'll be in touch. Was anything odd about what they told her? She was entitled to know actual events. Realities. Specifics of when, where, and how. They owed her that much.

Muscles involuntarily tightened in her gut.

She didn't have an answer, but maybe there was a purpose for her to go on living a little bit longer after all. If only for Dirk's sake to search out the truth. What had really happened to him? Where did it happen? Do they know who was responsible? A terrorist group, a psychotic individual? Maybe then she would be able to come to terms with to the reason Dirk's death. And the thought of finding out was something to live for.

She looked at all media reports she could find online. A small story about a car bombing appeared in Reuters. The BBC headline carried scant information about a reported incident happening on the border between Greece and Bulgaria. The ANA, Athens News Agency, gave little more specifics. Television and radio reports added small additional facts. And the Sofia, Bulgaria press had not yet even mentioned anything had happened.

In frustration, she pieced the bits of information together as best she could. Cora put together a rough sketch. It appeared a suicide bomber had approached a particular car heading toward the guarded border crossing.

Cora paced up and down, trying to fit these fragments together into an account that made sense. She sat at the table with her computer all night. She wrote questions to American journalistic sources, including The Washington Post, and The New York Times. She called the Athens local radio news station and questioned its reporters and editor. There was little more to add so far, they told her. She kept looking back to the screen, constantly surfing the internet, searching as many diverse sources as she could find. Russian, Israeli, Turkish.

Hours later, she woke up at the table, slumped over. A radio news report was beginning. *"Among those who had been held for questioning regarding the Parthenon explosion were several professors at the University of Athens. This morning they were released without charges. They held their fists high in spiteful defiance as Athens police looked on and held back crowds of both supporters and protestors..."*

A few names followed. One caught her attention, the known activist professor, Yiannis Petrakis. Hearing the name made her heart pound. She looked at the Athens photographs just released being shown online. She easily spotted Petrakis. Surrounded by police and lawyers, he was grinning widely. A hefty man with white thinning hair and a bulging stomach, he clasped both his hands tightly together above his head in a victory stance. He was clearly enjoying this moment of celebrity. 'You bastard,' she hissed, recalling Dirk's discussion of him and his boisterous boasts of terrorist ties.

The radio reporter continued. *"There are those that believe that Petrakis and his followers allegedly may have played a clandestine part in the recent Athens bombing, and perhaps their supporters might have had a role in yesterday's suicide bombing on the Bulgarian border..."*

She gasped. Was there a clear connection to the suicide bomber? Dirk's death? Petrakis or his devotees may have had a part.

She couldn't eat all day. The very thought of food made her nauseous. Lyra phoned. Her mother phoned. Her father phoned. She assured everyone she was alright for now, coping. She asked to be left by herself, at least for a bit. Not to come over for a day or two. She was managing. Despite qualms, they agreed.

Cora continued to make copious notes from the news reports.

It was intolerably difficult for her to begin to remove Dirk's personal belongings. Especially his clothing. Each shirt, each pair of slacks or jeans, sweaters, everything brought back some sweet memory or other. They had shared so much, developed so much to look forward to. An entire lifetime awaited.

Yet how could she remain here, in this home now? Alone. She saw Dirk everywhere. Since he had moved in with her it became a totally changed place. Could it ever go back to how it was? The way life had been before him. Could *anything* ever be the same? Of course not, she knew. Not ever. But what next? Late at night, while she sat sipping plain tea, her cell phone rang. It was an embassy number. She answered cautiously. "Yes?"

"Cora? This is Brian. Brian Downing. Are you all right?"

"I'm managing, Brian. I can't talk now. Call back in a few days."

"Don't hang up. Please. I have up-to-date information...I think it's only fair to let you know."

She sat up straight. "Information? What is it?"

"I can't talk from here. I can meet you somewhere. Anywhere you want."

"Now?"

"Yes. You'll want to hear me out, I promise."

"You can come over to our flat. I'm awake."

"Are you sure?"

"You said it's important."

"I have the address. A driver will bring me and wait. Give me half an hour."

She went to the kitchen to make more tea. Brian had never been here before. Dirk had asked her not to have much connection with him and she didn't understand why. Now she wondered if Dirk was concerned that Brian might know too many things going on he didn't want her to know.

Brian looked glum as she opened the door. He began to provide something of an apology, but Cora stopped him. "Come in, please," she said. "Sit down wherever you like."

He took a seat at the dining table, glancing at the pile of writings beside her computer. She brought a tray with two fresh cups of tea. "I have nothing else to offer." Placing one cup in front of Brian she sat herself opposite.

"Cora—"

She held up her hand to stop him. "I'm doing the best I can Brian. You don't need to feel bad for me." She folded her hands in front of her. "You said you wanted to talk. You have some things to tell me."

"The embassy is going to issue a public statement in the morning. And news organizations are going to run with it right away. I felt you had a right to know what's going on without having some TV or online site tell you."

"Thank you. I do appreciate that." She waited in silence. Brian cleared his throat and swallowed some of the tea. He tapped his fingers nervously.

"It's going to be disclosed that a diplomat from the American Embassy was purposely attacked by a suicide bomber approaching the Bulgarian border crossing with Greece. It was likely retribution for some recent terrorist arrests made in Bulgaria, they think. Demands for their release were ignored, so they decided to show the world they could act. The suicide bomber was presumed to be planning to set off his vest amid a crowd of cars packed by the border. A Bulgarian border guard apparently saw him and yelled to stop. The bomber knew which car our man was in and blew himself up on the driver's side. It was a quick and painless death. I can tell you that. The victim is being identified as a political officer on a special assignment."

"Go on."

"A terrorist cell with hidden branches here in Greece and other countries is believed to be behind the killing, we think. This faction hails from Chechnya. Old scores to settle, new violence to frighten innocent people. We believe the bomber was a nineteen- or twenty-year-old called Shamil Azizov. He and two older brothers are believed to have been radicalized by Al Qaeda zealots likely from Afghanistan. The eldest brother has been known to us for some time. He attended university here in Athens for a couple of years. Likely this is where he first became a revolutionary."

"Was he a student of that son of a bitch, Yiannis Petrakis?"

"I believe so, but that's unconfirmed. These groups have long tentacles and frequently collaborate with each other. Likely their cell was tipped off somehow, and they were seeking to discover any Americans working covertly. We've been involved in trying to gain insight into their agenda, their modes of operation. My personal guess is that Dirk got caught up in a counterespionage mess. Possibly he was already on their radar and might have been tracked for a while. We don't know specifics. But his death is their way of sending a strong message."

Cora stared at him blankly.

Brian started to reach his hand out to her but quickly pulled it back. "I shouldn't be telling you all this, but I think you deserve a few answers. Several months ago, one of our major contacts was assassinated in Istanbul. Our contact was a trusted informer. A member of a Chechen cell. A double agent, assisting us. He collaborated frequently with Dirk, providing solid information. His loss was a major blow. He'd provided prized intel for some time. He traveled back and forth regularly from Chechnya to Bulgaria and Turkey. Losing him cost us some vital data…"

"What is this you're telling me? I saw what went on. The embassy used Dirk like a lowly messenger boy. *Used* him. Dispatching him here and there, and everywhere like a courier. Meet with this one, meet that one. If he were stationed at his post in Athens, he'd still be alive. You make him sound like a CIA operative."

Brian's mouth opened. "Cora…He was."

She froze. Stunned. Chills ran up and down her spine. It wasn't possible. A spy? An operative at an embassy post? She wanted to protest, but her mind raced with memories of unexpected late-night calls, night flights, delays and more delays, then cleverly avoiding so many of her questions without explanation.

"Listen, Cora. I'm going to be transferred," Brian added. "They want me out of here now. My role has also been compromised. But I couldn't leave with a clear conscience at least without telling you these things so maybe one day you'd understand."

She drew a deep breath. A single tear fell. "I think I understand now. Both of you. When do you leave?"

"Tomorrow morning. Early."

She nodded. "Thank you for this. You're a decent man, Brian Downing."

He smiled thinly. "For the record, Brian Downing isn't my real name. It's one I've used since leaving the States. It happens a lot."

"Are…Are you hinting that Dirk's name was also an alias?"

"Dirk would have told you everything before your wedding. He did love you."

Her lips trembled and her eyes turned to pools.

Brian pushed back his chair and stood up. "Dirk was a lucky man. I envied him. You are quite a woman in your own right, Cora. God bless you wherever you go and whatever you do."

She got up and stood by the front door. He nodded to her. Then he left.

11

CORA SAT SPEECHLESS. DIRK HAD withheld so much. She hated him for it but still loved him with all her heart, that would never change. Whatever stupid things he had done were history now. He had paid the consequences dearly. So had she. His game with these dark demons had cost them both.

What now of her life, though? What next? She couldn't just sit there numb on the couch. She decided it would be best to resign her position as soon as possible. That was a no-brainer. And she certainly wasn't going to subject herself to the consolations of the judgmental staff at the embassy. Their solemn faces. Offers of friendship, support. Looking at her out of the corners of their eyes, shaking their heads at her misfortune. Living like that would be too painful, too filled with good memories to ever go back there now. Who would want to face all those people viewing her with their pity, condolences? Things could never be the same. What then should be the next step in her life? It was obviously too early for any decision—except a single one she now promised herself.

She started to make some calls. First to her shocked family, assuring them all she was dealing with the sad news well, needing solitude and a little time, and that she would come see them all in a few days. Their concern for her physical and emotional heath was genuine. Especially her father, whom she had to restrain from driving over immediately. She did her best to not sound as depressed and miserable as she was. Despite their qualms, they did as she asked, at least for now. That would not last, she knew. There was first one commitment to fulfil that gave her grief focus and purpose, and this next step must be done quickly.

The next phone call she made was to an old affiliate of her father who had worked in the export trade. He provided her with several other less successful contacts to look up regarding her vague questions. She spoke to each, enquiring about the port, about things sometimes brought in not quite listed on the official bill of lading.

"You don't want to do anything illegal," she was told.

"No, of course not. I'm making enquiries for a friend who's traveling abroad."

After a time, she was given a name she vaguely recognized. A businessman with something of a soiled reputation. A smalltime, shady cash only dealer who was said to provide merchandise overlooked by authorities. A nicer way of referring to him as a broker in contraband. He had a reputation for knowing the right folks to bribe on Athenian streets. People who for the right price would turn the other way. He was legally clean, it was said. Keeping his own hands out of it. No arrests, no records. But he was precisely the proper sort of contact for helping to find whatever someone might want.

She phoned the given number. The voice said, "Leave a message." Then a return call moments later said only to meet on a busy street corner at sunset. He would see if he could help. No promises. No guarantees. Her request was simple, but expensive. They called it a gift. That evening they met briefly, their talk taking barely a few minutes.

The price to fulfil her request was steep. Quality merchandise, she wanted. She would get it. Ready to use, as required. Cost for this gift: ten thousand euros. And then put an end to a poison.

Yes, she could raise that amount. Yes, it could all be delivered. At night. Near the docks by the Old Port. He knew a dilapidated onetime warehouse where they would meet. He would provide her with a proper address, directions she might require, that part would be easy. The item she was buying, though, needed to be managed with great care and caution. Did she understand that? She said she did. Good. A sole use for it. Then as soon as she could collect the cash and make payment, a colleague of his would be waiting at that warehouse to make the trade. If she had the money tomorrow, the gift would be ready tomorrow night.

She followed the bus routes from the university leading to the central areas of the city. Rain showers provided a suitable reason to wear Dirk's worn-out raincoat, with the collar drawn high. Old jeans. Old sneakers. Her hair was tightly pulled back in a short ponytail. She wore a shabby Greek fisherman's cap that when pulled down snugly hid eyebrows and part of her eyes. Dark glasses, a few careful smudges of muddied dirt concealed the shape of her cheekbones. She added small wads cotton wool between her gums and cheeks. She viewed herself in the mirror and smiled. She didn't recognize herself at all. She saw the image of a much older woman who appeared more a weary wharf worker than anything else.

She walked to the boulevard, along a street of pastel and brightly colorful homes, then turned and crossed the other way. She stood at the corners, waited for traffic lights. Then followed up a street one way, hurried through an alley, then casually strolled down another street. Learning the area, finding bus stops, routes to avoid, places to linger in shadows. Nearby bus stops. Nobody along the way seemed to take any notice.

When she approached the small balconied building she wanted, she crossed the street and leaned her shoulder against the stone wall of the building opposite. There she waited keenly watching the pink facade. It was still light, so she pretended to keep herself busy casually talking on her phone. There was no rush, she knew. If it took an hour, two hours, three, so what? If she had to return tomorrow, so what? Time was on her side.

This was a quiet tree-filled street. Upper middle class. Cars were parked on both sides of the road. As always, aromas of cooking meals infused the air. People began returning home from work. A well-dressed aging woman nodded at her. She politely nodded back. An elderly man using a cane approached. He used his key to open the front door, and she held it wide so he could enter easily without danger of tripping or falling. He thanked her politely for her assistance and entered the small lobby. She moved aside as the door shut and feigned walking away. She soon returned to the same spot. She checked the time. All daylight had diminished.

Streetlights shone in the dark. A sliver of a new moon hung above. She yawned, covering her mouth with her left hand, keeping her right hand in her pocket, holding the gift. A few more minutes passed. From the side of her vision, she saw headlights appear and then a car come to a hasty stop. Someone got out. A solitary figure. A man. He shut the car door, carrying a bag over his shoulder. It likely contained books and papers, but it caught her attention. Passing streetlights, he strode leisurely toward the building she was watching. Held against his chest by one arm was what appeared to be a grocery bag. There were bulky containers within, she could tell from its bulge, and perhaps a bottle of wine or two, and a baguette sticking out.

Cora put away the glasses and squinted. Her eyes fixated like a wolf on its prey. There were numerous photos of the notorious professor online, pictures she had carefully studied these past few days. A balding male, with white uncombed curly hair. He had a bulging belly that made him look pregnant under his sweater. He also groomed himself with about a three-day growth of stubble on his face. He was a perfect match with news pictures except he was much shorter than she had estimated.

She casually crossed the street between the cars and made her way to the front door of his building. She pretended to be searching for a name in the directory. He stood with his keys, opened the door, nodding to her. She smiled back and thanked him for holding the door for her. She let him walk in front of her to the elevator along the end of the wall. She stood back by the stairwell opposite. The elevator door began to open with no one in it.

"Professor Petrakis," she called. "Yiannis Petrakis!"

He turned his head sideways with a puzzled look.

With both hands she firmly held out her special gift. A shiny, brand-new Glock .45 G21 short-frame handgun with a fully loaded magazine. Simple, dependable, deadly.

His eyes grew wide. An arm went out toward her. "No, wait!"

She pulled the trigger. The ten-millimeter cartridges fired three times within a second. The recoil threw her off balance.

The back of his head exploded. Pieces of skull and brain and blood blasted across the elevator door, over the walls beside it. Petrakis fell to the ground in a heap. His stubby right hand twitched. The contents of his grocery bag spilled onto the cleanly washed stone floor. Oranges and fava beans rolled between his legs. The baguette looked fresh and tasty.

A door opened from the above floor.

Cora turned, walked briskly outside, down the street, into an alley and out the other side. Her heart was pounding so strongly she though it would burst. A nearby bus was ready to leave its stop. She stepped inside a moment before it pulled away. She pulled her hair loose and let it tumble to her shoulders. She took off the raincoat. Splatters of blood ran down the front and sleeves. She wrapped it like a parcel, with the expensive Glock inside a pocket. A few stops later she got off at a dark corner. Streetlight was minimal. In the distance she could hear the wail of an ambulance. She slowly ambled towards the water. When she reached the palisade railing, she took the gun and tossed it into the sea, sinking immediately. The raincoat she packed with nearby rocks and threw it into the water a bit further away. It splashed. She felt cold. Beyond tired, beyond exhaustion. There was no sense of triumph, no feeling of revenge. She had done what someone should have done years before. Yiannis Petrakis would warp the minds of no more students.

12

LYRA HAD PHONED NUMEROUS TIMES that day. There was no answer. She grew increasingly worried, anxious that Cora might have hurt herself, or worse, taken her own life. She phoned her father, asked him to leave work right away and drive them both to Cora's flat. She had a key to be used in case of emergencies. Her senses told her this was that time.

They were there. Lyra cautiously opened the door with her key. The front room was dim and deserted, curtains and shutters were pulled tightly. It looked as though no one was home. A small whimpering sound came from the bedroom. There in the corner Cora sat on the floor, knees up, arms wrapped around them.

Lyra crossed herself. Her father ran to her side and leaned beside her. Cora seemed unaware he was there. There were no fresh tears. Only multiple dried streaks running down her pallid face onto her white blouse.

"We need to call an ambulance," said Lyra.

"No," replied the family patriarch, Zander Drakos, in a voice that no one disobeyed. "We'll bring her home."

They helped her up and Cora followed limply as they left. Lyra guided her into the back seat, then ran around to sit beside and hold her tightly. It was a while before anyone spoke.

At length, Cora turned her face toward her older sister. Her father observed from the mirror as he drove. "I killed him," she said, the words almost choking from her lips. "I killed that bastard Petrakis."

"Mother of God," panted Lyra. "Why? Why in heaven—"

"He deserved it. He was responsible for Dirk's death."

"He what?" cried Lyra.

"She doesn't know what she's saying," said Zander, paying attention to the road. "She must have heard some news or other on the television. Can't you see she's upset and confused. Some nationalist fanatics are responsible, I heard."

"No, Papa, it was me. I did it. I killed him. I bought a gun. An immensely powerful gun."

Her father now grew tense. Was it possible? Did she really realize what she was saying?

"Cora, listen to me. It's not easy to learn to shoot a gun. You need to train for it. Take pistol lessons."

She shook her head vehemently. "All I had to do was pull the trigger. It was loaded. All set up and ready for me. Unlocked. It fired so easily."

"What kind of gun?" Zander was becoming increasingly concerned.

"A Glock 21, short frame pistol."

The car swerved to the left and quickly corrected. A Glock was a top quality, expensive, high-powered weapon, he understood. It indeed fitted the description of the kind of weapon that took off half of the professor's skull. There were pictures of the collapsed body in the newspapers, on the computer, everywhere. Only the disfigured face was blackened out.

"She needs a hospital…"

"No hospital! We're taking her home. We'll be keeping her safe, understand?"

"What about the police?" The thought made Lyra turn ashen. "They have no clues," snapped Zander. "Cora stays with us, at least for now. Until she begins to heal. Understood? Then we'll all learn the truth."

Cora's mother, Annella, greeted them at the door. Zander and Lyra slowly walked and eased Cora across the room. Annella bit her lower lip hard and struggled to retain her composure at the sight of her daughter.

Zander helped Cora into the guestroom that used to be her bedroom. In the kitchen Annella boiled hot tea and bullion soup. Plain toast was offered. Cora sat up on the side of her bed and held a single piece of toast in her hand. At Lyra's urging she took several bites.

"No one is to be told Cora is here," Zander said firmly. "No discussions. The few people I might trust I'll deal with myself. As far as everyone else is concerned, we haven't heard from or seen her. Not even others in the family. No uncles, no cousins. We're worried too, tell anyone who asks. Right now, reports say the police think rival terrorist gangs or national extremist groups were likely responsible for the killing. Let's hope their line of thinking remains that way."

"Cora could become a suspect because of Dirk." Lyra said.

The patriarch scratched at the side of his long face. "Possibly. But for now, they have no reasons or direct ties. That horrid little man had lots of enemies to keep the police busy investigating. I expect the American Embassy to get itself involved, you can be sure. We have to keep them at bay, let them ask all the questions they want. We play stupid. Could she have run away, fearful of Dirk's killers? We can demand some answers. The Americans will be concerned, but helpless eventually. Any terrorist group from Iran to Iraq, to Afghanistan could have done this as revenge against other rivals. Eventually, though, you're right. Our own police will want to have her questioned."

"We need to keep her safe at any cost," said Lyra. "From everyone. You can see the kind of pain she's in."

"Of course, we do. Find her mobile phone and get rid of it. No contact. We can't trust who might call or who she may want to talk to. Lyra, type a letter of resignation to the embassy, Cora will sign it. Leave all her things in her flat exactly as they are. It will look like she's fled in a hurry. Gone somewhere, some private place where she can't be located. But we can't keep her here at home, either. As soon as possible we have to get her far away from Athens."

"We can drive up to the Larissa villa, Papa. Perfect for Mama to take care of her there. She can go tomorrow. Quietly, without anyone aware."

Annella nodded. "I can do the drive. You go to work tomorrow. Zander. Like normal. An ordinary day. Cora needs to heal. It takes time."

The villa outside the town of Larissa in Thessaly would provide a good short-term refuge. Nestled near the Peneus River, not far from the Aegean Sea, it offered comfort and a safe temporary haven. And at this time of year the locale would still be quiet before the usual onslaught of summer tourists. No local villagers would look twice at a few members the Drakos family arriving. The secluded villa had been held by the family for several generations. Away from roads, surrounded by orchards and olive groves, it provided excellent privacy from prying eyes.

"For a little while, our villa can offer good shelter. But it's best to get her far away. Somewhere where no one can identify her. Outside of the country. Entirely away from Greece."

"You think she should run away? Disappear somewhere?"

Zander looked at his wife and eldest daughter. "Not run away. Leave. Emigrate. What choices do we have? The day will come when she'll be questioned. Her connections to the American Embassy and her American fiancé killed by terrorists will draw a straight line eventually. Hellenic anti-terrorist police operate in independent ways. They might even accuse Cora as being a part of some deranged reactionary group. Who can say? You know what she's done." Even as he spoke the words seemed surreal to them all.

"So, we whisk her away, just like that? To where, Papa?"

"Let me think. I have people I can talk to, the right kind with knowledge of these situations. We might need to get her a new passport. Even using a different name." He turned to Annella. "Your cousin, Orestis. He has those sorts of connections in Istanbul and in Sophia."

"Orestis is a criminal. You know his sleazy past. You want to deal with him and his underworld associates? Pay to him procure a forged passport for our daughter?" He was known to receive lucrative fees for composing fake work permits and visas for asylum seekers and illegal immigrants. Annella was astounded that Zander would consider it.

Zander grimaced. "And if she stays here and the police come asking questions? Heaven forbid our daughter should be arrested, put on public trial and then sent to prison...for murder. Could she endure that? Would that be better?"

Annella remained silently overcome.

"It would kill Mama—" Lyra stopped mid-sentence.

Hearing Zander's words made the crime seem all too real. "Let's not panic. We'll find a satisfactory solution, I promise. Meanwhile we all need to stay calm and evaluate our next move."

"What were you saying about a forged passport?" Cora was standing at the opened door of her bedroom. She appeared less dazed.

"Go back to bed. You need to rest, eat a little food. Later we'll all talk."

"You're talking about me, aren't you?"

Her father went over and gently took Cora back to her room. She didn't resist. He eased her down and she rested on the bed.

"We'll bring you a tray soon. Try to eat whatever you can." Across the room photographs of her childhood stood placed atop a dresser. He glanced at them and gently kissed her forehead. At this moment Cora seemed very much like the little girl he had raised. Now, he vowed to do everything possible to restore her to the woman she had become.

Before dawn Annella drove off with Cora. Four hours later they arrived at the villa. Zander also had a trusted worker follow to help take care of them.

Anti-terrorist police continued to comb Athens and the countryside. The bullets used were easy to identify. Rumors spread that they were looking for a lone shooter, while others speculated on perhaps a trio of assassins, one waiting in a car while the others followed the professor into the lobby of his building. Because it was dark there were no eyewitnesses. One man however, an elderly book dealer who lived across the street, reported that an unknown working-class woman had held his door for him. He said the woman appeared to be waiting for someone at the house where the professor lived.

These bits of possible information kept public speculation churning. Zander realized it wouldn't be long before the police would come questioning the American Embassy translator who had been engaged to the terrorist victim.

He met with Orestes. Giving as little information as possible he made the transaction to acquire a new passport with Cora's altered ID. A slight change in surname, a minor alteration of birthday and birth year. The deal was for cash, payment required on delivery. Zander provided a passport photo of Cora, no explanation given, none asked.

Getting her safely away would be trickier. Zander decided that Lyra and Cora would travel together to Cyprus, perhaps by boat. No passport check was required among fellow European Union nations. Then, after a few days of rest at a hotel in Nicosia, Lyra and Cora would board a short flight to Egypt. Cairo's huge international airport would provide an easier place from which to depart for America without too many questions. Unlikely she would be probed or identified by Egyptian authorities with the same tenacity as agents in Athens. Her new passport with slight identity alterations appeared perfect. Visas and any other necessary documents would now be easier to obtain.

The price for the passport delivery was steep, and within a week the finished product was delivered by hand. Zander inspected it scrupulously; it was faultless. A perfect forgery. He placed it carefully into his inside jacket pocket and on Sunday drove to the villa. Once there, he could discuss Cora's condition and ability to travel. Cora was undoubtedly improving, Lyra assured her father, but it was going to take time to heal, and a lengthy process until she would fully recover. Zander knew this was true, but at the same time he also knew that time was working against them.

Cora was eating better, but she had visibly lost weight. Lyra remained apprehensive. She would walk with Cora, taking her to the olive groves and picturesque surrounding farmlands to spend time amid nature's magical curative powers.

One afternoon they drove to the sea. They sat atop a great rock where they used to go as children and stared out at the blue waters. Cora basked in the fresh sea breezes, fondly remembering this place and those times of happiness, when the world seemed a gentler and kinder place. Filled with flowers and sunshine. Laughter. Friends and family gathered together. Sweet evenings when the adults drank ouzo, and the younger ones sang and played games.

They sat in silence for a long while when Lyra finally spoke. "It's better not holding things inside the way you do," she said, her hand delicately touching over Cora's heart. "I know it's difficult. I understand. But open up to me, please. Share your feelings, share how this happened." There was a plea in her eyes.

Cora remained quiet for a while. Lyra had decided to say nothing more, when Cora blurted, "I was in such a terrible state those first days. I honestly don't know how I survived. So alone, so frightened." She wept. Lyra sat and listened. Cora sniffed and blew her nose into an offered a tissue. "I knew he was dead, knew Dirk had died because of some demented fanatic's need to blow others up along with himself. I felt I needed to find out more. Who did this? Why, why? Late at night there was a knock on the door. It was a friend from the embassy. A man who collaborated closely with Dirk. A close colleague, called Brian. He came to share some information, he said. He was going to be transferred from Athens the next day, he told me, and he wanted me to know some things before he left. Brian's words turned my whole life inside out. He told me that Dirk's position at the embassy wasn't just a political officer, a valuable assistant to the ambassador. His real job was working for the CIA. That was his true role. Brian did the same, I realized. And more than that, Brian said his name was an alias, hinting maybe Dirk's was also." Lyra's eyes widened. Her mouth opened slightly. "It's possible Dirk left without me even knowing his real name.

"Brian assured me Dirk's love was real, though. That he would have explained everything before our wedding. And he honestly tried to ease my pain. I know he meant well. But…" she broke down and sobbed. Lyra pulled her close and let the tears flow, let the poisons Cora was holding inside come pouring out. She needed to rid herself of this torment, this awful sorrow.

"So, I ask," Cora continued after a time, "how can I ever know the truth? I feel so angry Dirk made me doubt who I am. What's real, what wasn't? There I was, a trusting, naïve young woman, turned into a self-doubting, blithering, helpless fool. Like a character in some film, only the character was me."

She stopped, looked away and wiped her bloodshot eyes. She laughed a short bitter laugh. "After his death all I could think of was that spiteful, hate-mongering professor who taught malleable students subversion and terrorism. To become 'freedom fighters' for causes they don't even understand. Dirk had mentioned this evil man, and how by spewing his venom he radicalized so many. Recruiting terrorists was his primary function. And I when I learned the idiot suicide bomber had been a student and acolyte of Petrakis, I lost all my bearings, even my sense of reason. The only thing keeping me sane was stopping this man. Ending his life, ending the spread of his vile ideology. Me, this rational, moral person. I knew some people to contact. The right kind of people that Papa had spoken of in business dealings. So, I got the money together. Money saved or given to me, and I paid the price for the right kind of weapon. It didn't matter Petrakis wasn't the one who detonated the bomb. To me he was responsible. He murdered Dirk and robbed me of my future life. For that, I vowed to end his. But I know what I did demands a price."

She looked at her staring sister in reflection. "Yes, I was aware of what I was doing, even in my twisted frame of mind. But now, I close my eyes and I see the blood and skull splattered over walls, over his lifeless body. I committed murder, Lyra. Murder." Cora broke down again, and Lyra continued to hold her until the sun edged low on the horizon, and it was time to go.

During the following days Cora remained quiet and introspective, but her appetite was improving, she stood straighter, and began speaking in her normal voice.

Zander knew time was getting shorter. Questions and speculation about the mysterious woman noticed by the old bookseller grew more intense. Finding others responsible for the killing seemed to be going nowhere. Nor did any group proudly declare responsibility. The Greek police were expanding their search. The 'lone wolf' theory was gaining attention. Zander, Annella, and Lyra realized the time for a decision was at hand.

Annella remembered another relative, a maternal cousin named Eleni, who had immigrated to America some decades earlier. She had married a Greek man in America named Karas Padnos, himself a recent immigrant. Sadly, Eleni Padnos had passed away a few years before after a lengthy illness. Karas Padnos was a businessman who owned a restaurant in New York, it was said. Annella's family had spoken well of him. Several had met him during a visit to Eleni, and they also spoke well of him. Now nicknamed Gus by all, he was said to be industrious and trustworthy, and although not a man of formal education, he was nevertheless a respected member of various Greek organizations located in New York.

Zander and Annella discussed the idea privately and quietly. They also made enquiries from other relatives living in America about this man. Replies came back favorable.

Upon returning to Athens, Zander phoned Gus Padnos in New York with a proposition. Annella was a cousin of his late wife, Eleni. They were related by marriage, thus remained family despite Eleni's passing, for which he gave condolences. Gus was appreciative and was familiar with the distinguished family name Drakos, of which that Zander was now the patriarch.

Zander told him he had a worrisome problem. His younger daughter, a young woman in her twenties, had been through a recent tragedy. A terrible, unfortunate loss of life of a man she had loved. An American. Her heart was broken. She needed to heal, and to begin a new life. America would be a perfect place. Would it be possible for Karas 'Gus' Padnos to help his daughter Cora if she came to live in New York? Could he assist in finding a way for her to start life over? She also needed to find a place to live, perhaps also a job? Zander was willing to pay whatever costs and fees were required. It was a big favor, he acknowledged, but Zander's gratitude to Karas 'Gus' Padnos would be sealed forever. Cora's sister and mother would come and visit regularly, and perhaps one day in the future Cora might return to Athens. But not now. That was not possible. It was necessary for her to stay away.

"I understand you perfectly," Gus said in response, recognizing there was more to the story than told. "It will my honor to fulfill your request."

"Thank you with all my heart." Zander replied, truly appreciative and comforted. His daughter would be safe, and well cared for.

Then, as businessman to businessman, he assured the restaurant owner that any help Karas might need financially Zander would be there to help. His word was his bond.

Karas listened sympathetically and felt authentic compassion for the young girl who had lost her loved one. Zander was a man to be respected and admired. If not family by blood, he still was family. He promised he would keep his word and do whatever he could. Gus suggested she live with his widowed sister at first, and he could also give her work in his restaurant, if she wanted. And Gus added that he was grateful for the generous business offer, even though it was not necessary. But if any unforeseen need ever arose, he would gladly accept. As honorable man to man, as family-linked Greek to Greek, Karas 'Gus' Padnos gave his own word of honor. Send the girl when she was ready. What was the daughter's name again? Cora. Ah, yes. Cora. When would she arrive?

The date and time were given, she would arrive on a connecting flight from Cyprus to Cairo, then directly fly to New York. Karas Padnos guaranteed he would have his best employee waiting for her at Kennedy International Airport all night if necessary. He once more assured the anxious father that he would personally take responsibility in seeing his Cora would begin a fresh, good life in America.

13

CORA ARRIVED IN THIS STRANGE new world with only a single suitcase. The immigration officer was brisk but polite. Her passport was scanned. Cora held her breath. It was not flagged. After a few cursory questions, at which Cora replied she was there to visit with family and tour, the inspector said, "Welcome to the United States, Ms. Drakos. Enjoy your stay."

Amid the tumult and confusion of passengers scurrying to collect baggage, locate flights of friends and family, Cora was able to locate the driver that Karas Padnos had sent. They spoke in Greek. Her driver worked for Karas. He explained that here Karas was known to everyone as Gus. He chuckled as he told her the nickname was acquired years ago, and no one quite remembered how it happened.

"But I've never met him. What do I call him, then?" she asked, slightly confused. "Karas? Mr. Padnos?"

"Just call him Gus. He'll be delighted. You'll see."

Cora stared out the backseat window. She saw jammed highways and countless thoroughfares in every direction. Crowded two- and three-story houses and towering apartment buildings on either side. Multiple stores, bridges, cemeteries, trains. Short trees, tall trees. Even a glimpse of a bit of forest surrounded by homes. A totally different landscape, a boundless infrastructure unlike anything she was familiar with, in a totally different world. The pain of Dirk remained, and her sadness endured. However, her inner turbulence had begun to fade, and she felt she was turning a corner, a beginning in returning to normal. The time recuperating in Thessaly with Lyra and her parents had been a blessing after the tragedy. By no means had she healed, but she realized she was mending. Less fractured, more in control. Plus, a tinge of excitement of being in America buoyed her mood.

New York City contained five counties, called boroughs, she was told. This was one, known as Queens, was the location of the Athena Diner. The location where both Gus and his sister lived, though in different homes and neighborhoods. She was being taken to his sister's house now. Irene, a widow, was a similar age as Cora's own mother.

Tears fell from Irene's eyes when Cora arrived. The overweight, oval-faced woman hugged Cora tightly telling her she was welcome to stay forever. Waiting in the living room was the man to whom she knew she already owed so much: Karas Padnos. Gus. He stood beaming, a big, tall man with oversized hands on his hips, and shoulders as broad as a refrigerator. He took her hands in a brotherly fashion and welcomed her warmly. She fumbled with what to call him, and he laughed boisterously. "Everybody calls me Gus. *Everybody*. Please, I'd like you to as well."

"Thank you, Gus. Thank you for taking this chance on me."

"Life is filled with chances, Cora. Maybe God placed them there for us to decide. Rest here with Irene as long as you want. When you're ready, I'll bring you to the Athena Diner. I call it my American child."

For several weeks Cora found small ways to reconcile this new world with her old life and the life ahead. Meanwhile both Irene and Gus introduced her to New York. A nighttime car ride revealed for her the enormity, wealth, and greatness of this unrivaled city. To see it in films was one thing, but to view it in front of her eyes was another. The immense Hudson River spilling into the vast Atlantic Ocean, a boat ride circling the island of Manhattan. When they walked, she was astounded at the frantic pace of life, the noisy subways below, the buses, taxis, and cars above, plus the crowds upon crowds filling the streets everywhere. She now realized how much her life was going to change, but to what extent and in how many ways she could never have fathomed.

Gus showed her everything about his diner, and she willingly agreed to take a job. Not just any job, he stressed. He wanted her to learn everything. For a time, she served as a hostess, then as a waitress in training. A few weeks after he put her into the kitchen as a helper to the dishwashers. A morning shift, then a late-night shift. After that to work with the line cooks. Hot, sweaty work. Most difficult at mealtimes of breakfast, lunch, and dinner. After becoming a breakfast cook and standing over the stoves for a while, she was given the task of bringing in each day's early morning delivered produce, examining it, cleaning it, remonstrating with the different vendors about quality when necessary. Orders bought from bakeries were given for her to inspect. Dessert was a vital part of every meal. Gus demanded the finest quality cakes and pies, and she was given the task of determining if anything was not quite fresh enough to meet his standards.

At other times she was given the task of mopping the shiny linoleum tile floors. And she cleaned the restrooms too, Men's Rooms and Ladies Rooms. She cleaned tables with the busboys, reset them for the next day, took her share of tips at the end of the night. Making sure the trash was properly collected from the many bins and huge heavy bags in the back was assigned to her as well. Just another necessary part of restaurant cleanliness.

Working the cash register was easy enough, but when it came time to tally the books each night with the day's receipts she had to work slowly and carefully. Making sure that payment was correct, that cash was deposited after hours, that credit cards were properly overseen, and receipts correctly given. Of course, the staff had to be paid, and their tips split evenly, giving a reasonable share of them to the busboys. The books needed to be reconciled for tax time every quarter, and he patiently taught her how, then sat and smilingly drank coffee while he watched her struggle on her own. She made sure accounts were complete and prepared for the diner's accountant to reconcile. She got used to hearing different members of staff calling out, "Hey Gus!" seeking answers and his assistance during various times of day and night.

Many months later Gus announced that he was satisfied. Cora proved to be a good learner with a quick mind, and fast on her feet. It was then that late one evening he asked her to remain with him after all the staff had gone home. They sat at a quiet booth in a corner near the swinging kitchen doors.

"Running a restaurant isn't easy, is it?" he said quietly.

"No, it's not."

"But it gets in your blood, doesn't it?"

She looked at him. "It can if you own it. If you run it well."

"Do I run it well?'

"You're a champion, Gus. You know that. I doubt anyone could do a better job than you."

He leaned forward and met her gaze. "You could, Cora."

"Me? No, not like you, Gus."

"I think you can." He leaned back easily and sipped from a carbonated bottle of water. "I want to have a serious talk with you, Cora. Is now a suitable time, or are you too tired? I can drive you home and we can talk tomorrow."

Inquisitive, she said, "I am tired, but now would be fine. What is it you want to discuss?"

Normally never short of words, Gus sought what he wanted to say. "I've watched you from the first day you arrived. You may not know it, but you impressed me from the very first day. When I put you to work, I thought you would learn the way everyone does. But you surprised me with your abilities. I have no doubt you could run the Athena Diner like this." He snapped his fingers. "I admire you."

"You're giving me too much credit, Gus."

"No. I've watched you carefully. I've seen how you're able to switch from task to task with no complaints. I bet you were equally good in Athens."

She looked down at her hands. "You don't know me. Or my past. The things that happened in my life. Difficult things, Gus."

"I know enough. More than you think."

She shook her head. "No. Gus. You don't."

He placed a compassionate hand on top of hers. "I recognized your grief when you arrived. And your father mentioned the American you were going to marry. I know he worked at the American Embassy, and died horribly in a terror attack…"

Tears welled. "Yes. He was an amazing man. What happened wasn't fair. But of course, life isn't fair. But there's more to the story. More that happened."

"Shhh, Cora." He stopped her from saying anything else. "I'm more aware than you realize. Listen to me, Cora. Let me tell you a few things about my life. I'd like to share with you."

"I know you loved your wife very much."

"Yes, but not that. My earlier life, in Greece. I want you to know."

She agreed. She used a tissue to dry her eyes and blow her nose. She sat straight, arms folded.

"I was born in Cyprus, in a poor area of Nicosia workingmen. My father left to find work on the mainland and never came back. My older brothers took care of the family. I had little formal schooling. I wanted to learn things, but my family had no money, so they couldn't send me to schools to study. So when I was fourteen, I worked for passage on a freighter. I wasn't interested in becoming a sailor, and certainly not a fish-erman, like so many who break their backs. I came to Athens for a time, and found myself working in kitchens. When I was lucky, they made me a waiter. An easier job, less grease and sweat. There was little to earn, but I saved my wages, ate from leftovers at the tables, shared a room with three other hungry kids. But I learned. I watched them all, cooks and cleaners, bosses and floor sweepers. Saw what needed to be done. My plan was to go maybe to Crete to try and start a tiny place of my own." He paused, clearly recalling those challenging times and hopeful dreams.

"I was big and strong. By eighteen I was powerful. I could fight a bull. That type of man. A friend of mine told me he knew a way for us to make some quick and good money. There was a lot of interest in fighting back then. You know, like on the television. Prizefighters, boxers. I was bulky but fast. I also learned to wrestle. There were local wrestling matches being held illegally in barns and farms, and even on the streets. Local people loved it. To watch. To see blood. They drank, shouted, and cursed. Fighting drew crowds. And betting. I found a man to be my manager. An old, retired fighter who loved the game and was willing to teach me for a small piece of the action. So, I fought. 'Karas the King,' they called me in wrestling. A stupid name. My friend always bet our money on me, and I almost always won. But it was small time cash. And dangerous. There were no doctors to take care if a man broke his bones or suffered worse injuries inside his body. The big money was in boxing. You know, like the great American champions that everybody looked up to and admired. I trained. Sacks of grain and beef became my punching bags. I was still young. Almost nineteen. Boxing gloves, I bought the best kind. Practiced in cheap gyms in Athens and sometimes on the streets in a few other towns. Some professionals took note. Scouts said I had some talent. This boy is tough and big. Hard to bring down, harder to knock out. And my new friends announced that I was ready to become a true professional."

Cora was intrigued at the story. She listened intently.

"I won five fights in a row. I knocked out two professional fighters. It was a surprise, even to me. More people took notice. My picture and name appeared a few times in the papers. A new champion is here in Greece! Karas Padnos! My head grew large. I could become a European champion, I told myself. My name would be known throughout Greece—beyond even. Maybe in Italy next, then France. Who could say? Oh, I had my share of bruises and pain, plenty, but now I was beginning to earn good money. I had lots of friends, gourmet food, ouzo, and women. Life was good. After another few bouts, the boxing league set me against a known fighter, someone also said to have a chance of becoming great. I had heard of him. A nobody like me. A kid from slums like me. People talked about the upcoming fight. I was ruthless, the papers said, but so was my opponent. It would be an epic event. Tickets were sold out in days. We were both powerful, both tall and strong. An even match."

Here Gus paused. His mouth contorted, his lips trembled. "The fight began. A legitimate boxing ring. An honest referee and judges. More than a thousand people were there to watch. The bell for round one rang. At first, we danced around each other. Boxers studying each other, looking for weaknesses. He missed a blow, I missed several. The round ended. I was pleased. I could beat him, I sensed it. I was stronger, faster. Let him wear himself out, I told myself. Let him grow tired. Then I will strike." Gus took several deep breaths and went on. "My strategy worked. I tried to take it as easy as I could while he punched and punched while I protected myself. In the sixth round I saw my chance. He was becoming slower, weary. When his punch missed my jaw, I hit him on the side of his head with my powerful right hand. Then with my left an uppercut against his jaw, and another blow to the side of his head. He fell to the ground. People screamed and many clapped their hands. I went to my corner. The referee counted to ten. I had won. My opponent tried to rise but I saw he couldn't. There was blood on his face—both our faces—but his was worse, much worse. He got to his knees and looked about him. Dazed of course, but more than that. He shouted something. His manager came running with the doctor. They brought a stretcher while I was being announced as the winner. But I felt no joy, no pride. What had happened? How much did I hurt him?"

Gus got up and got himself a bottle of soda. He drank it all at once then returned to face Cora.

"He…He couldn't see. This poor boy was not able to see anything. They took him to a hospital. His eyes, God have mercy, my fists took his eyes…"

"You blinded him?"

Gus hung his head and nodded. She thought she would never witness this tough man cry, but now he did.

"Yes. My blows to his head. I did severe damage to his optic nerve. Severe damage. A few days later I tried to reach out to his family. I offered them my winnings. I told them I would go to church and pray. They refused my money. His wife sobbed. She had children. I didn't know that. There was an official enquiry into our fight. It had been legitimate, it was ruled. If anything, the referee should have stopped the fight earlier because my opponent's eye was already badly bleeding. I was not to blame. But of course, I was, Cora. I took away his sight. Took it forever. I could fight no more. Never. My heart sank. I prayed and prayed. To no avail. I stopped fighting. Finished. Done with this horrible thing. This was not the life I had sought. I wanted to run away anywhere. A few people spat when my name was mentioned. My dreams were over. That was when I decided to come to America. A new life, to put aside the old one. Since then, I have had money sent to his family every month. Not in my name, but they know. I think he sees a little with one eye now. I pray so, but I have never forgotten. I came to New York by boat, with no papers. It's then I started to work manually. Now only twenty years old and I was still young and strong. But deep down I live with the knowledge and regret that I had blinded a decent man forever."

Cora sat stunned.

"So, you see, we all carry heavy weights upon our shoulders. You have yours, but you are not alone."

"I am so sorry for what happened, Gus. I feel for you, and for him too. I wish I could be helpful, but I don't think I can."

"Yes, you can." His deep voice turned stronger.

"How?"

"One day you will take over the Athena Diner. You will run it and then you will own it."

She looked at him questioningly. "What are you saying?"

"I am going to make you a manager starting next week. A light shift at first. Under my supervision, then in a while you'll be on your own."

"I can't do that. You don't understand."

"It will pay more money. Enough for you own apartment if you want."

"I'm flattered, Gus. Really, I am. But there's so much you don't know about me. And I doubt I can ever fully speak of it."

"There have been stories from back home that come to me. I know that weeks before you arrived in America some crazy professor at the university was killed. They said he might have had something to do with the murder of the American from the embassy."

She tensed, said nothing.

"But then, it's only talk." He shrugged his wide shoulders. "The man perhaps was responsible for much grief in the world. I have no respect for evil doers."

Cora took the hand he offered and held it. "What is it you want, Gus?"

"The truth?"

"Please."

"I have never spoken about this to anyone. Not even my sister. Not too long ago I began having pain. Down my arms, in my chest. I learned that I have a heart condition. Right now, thank the heavens, everything remains under control. I take my medicine, and I see the doctor for regular visits. They run tests, take my blood, ask me questions." He spoke with an aura of melancholy and acceptance.

Cora sniffed, put the back of her hand under her nose, and looked directly at him. "I'll learn to take over and run the diner smoothly for you. You won't have to worry. And you won't have to work so hard. I will become your manager. Your eyes and ears here whenever you have to leave to go somewhere."

He waited to say his next words. "And, Cora, I also offer you, my name."

She was taken aback. "What?"

"My name to become your name too. A new life for you, for me, to share. My life has been lonely for a long time. It's time for me to have someone. You know I care for you. For you, it would also be a life with American citizenship, and an American passport. You may remain Cora Drakos forever, but if you ever want to travel home, no one will recognize you with your new name. I am saying I want you to be my wife. I am more than twenty years older than you. I realize you can never love me the way you did with your American. But that's not what I am looking for. I need a companion. A partner. Perhaps in a little time you may find some affection for me in your heart. But if not, I accept that. And if…"

"And if…what?"

"And if God calls me, whatever I have will be yours. My sister Irene could never take over the restaurant. I want it for you. For you alone. That is what I want."

14

HUNTER CALLED CORA AS SOON as he got to work and opened his computer.

'Hey, give me a visit when you can. I just received info from CODIS. The Combined DNA Index System. You'll be wanting to hear about it."

Cora gave instructions to Eddie Coltrane in the morning about covering for her at the diner. She straightened her dress and combed her hair, waving to Sarah Sweeny at the cash register as she left.

In less than five minutes she was at the door of the police precinct. To her surprise Jonah Hunter was standing in front. He was leaning over a police cruiser, speaking with the driver. Several patrol cars were lined up behind, ready to roll. When he saw her, he cut short his conversation. Two uniformed officers crossed the narrow street holding coffee cups. "Morning, Mrs. Gus," each said. She smiled and waved. Regular customers walking back from the diner.

"You got here quickly," Hunter said, putting out a hand.

Cora took it. "You look pleased with yourself, Detective," she replied.

"Best day I've had since my ex-wife turned over my share of our house on Long Island." Hunter had been divorced some years earlier. A veteran of the long grim war in Afghanistan, he had returned suffering from PTSD. With time and good counseling, he was able to resume normal life, but his marriage never fully recovered. Working in the Military Police gave him an inside track with the NYPD. Since joining the force his career became his life, and he was good at it.

"Should we come upstairs to my office or take a walk, Mrs. Gus?"

Cora looked at him. "You know, I've often said you can call me Cora. That's my name."

He chuckled. "Seems like the world calls you Mrs. Gus. But okay. Cora. I like it. My office good?"

"Sure, Hunter."

They walked up the dusty stairs and into the detective rooms. Hunter offered a seat and he called up a page on his computer. "Civilians don't get to see this stuff very often," he said.

"I'm honored."

They both grew serious. "The hospital records on the night of the beating are limited on details other than medical procedures. However, blood was drawn on our 'John Doe,' called 'Mitch,' and sent to a lab for evidence of HIV or any of the Covid viruses. Let me show you." Cora peered at the screen. Blood test results on a multitude of indicators.

Hunter scrolled down two pages.

"Blessed are the men and women of serology. They extract genomic DNA from whole blood. A cell-free technology plus. I put the results they sent through the FBI labs, and for all records available to federal law enforcement agencies across the country."

"Isn't that for perpetrators, not victims?"

"Sure—unless the victim also has his own criminal record neatly filed away. Let me show you what I found."

She read a few lines about an arrest in Seattle some fifteen years ago. An assault with a knife outside a bar. "A very common crime," Hunter explained. "Claimed self-defense. Found guilty of an 'A' misdemeanor. Prosecution wanted it bumped up to a more serious violation, but the judge was lenient. He was sentenced to one year in a medium facility. He got out in seven months."

Cora looked at the police photo of the convicted assailant, studying the face carefully. Behind the cold stare, disheveled hair and stubble were gentle features. Missing from his mugshot was an angry defiant expression often seen in such photos.

"Now take a look at this," said Hunter. "California, nearly thirty years ago."

"Hit and Run," Cora read out loud. "San Luis Obispo, California. A car speeding from Morro Bay. A woman walking to the hospital where she worked was run over and died at the scene. The car didn't stop. It was found by the California Highway Patrol early the next morning at a motel in Atascadero. Located about twenty miles from the crime scene. Car was a black BMW, expensive. Dented with spots of blood on the fender and front left light."

"Go on, there's more."

"The driver was intoxicated. Alcohol level more than double the limit. Traces of cocaine too. He'd been at a party the night before. Drinking, girls, sniffing coke. He took off before dawn because he didn't want to arrive late for some important meeting…" Cora frowned and sighed. "Let me see his police photo."

Hunter enlarged the photograph. It was certainly the same man as the Seattle photo. Disheveled. The same man, though. Much younger. Handsome and clean cut.

"Here's what really caught my attention," said Hunter. "Some thirty years ago, when I was just finishing college, I liked sports. You heard Father Marcel and me talk about tennis, remember?"

She nodded.

"This guy, the driver. His name is Alan Connery. Alan Mitchell Connery. A tennis pro. I mean a professional player. Talented and becoming known.

He'd won a few important matches in pro tournaments. He was poised to be seeded. Ranked on the strength of prior wins. This guy was good, Cora. *Real* good." Hunter went over to the coffee pot atop a counter. He poured himself a cup of black, no sugar, and offered one to Cora. She took hers black too, sipping while Hunter continued.

"Reading this history jarred my memory. I do remember that name, that case. He was all-court, meaning he played all styles, serve and volley, learned how to throw opponents off balance. In short, a young man from a good family, going places. With a real chance to be a big star."

"He blew it with his drinking and partying?"

"Big time. He'd been a ball boy as a kid. Retrieving balls for the players and giving them back. He had a real in with tennis pros. His dad had money. The kid learned to play at their home tennis court, plus a pro teacher. I mean, he had it made."

She held the coffee cup near her lips. "I can guess the rest. Spoiled. Got whatever he wanted."

"Sure. But you gotta work hard to become a real tennis pro. This guy really loved the game. That stupid hit and run ruined his life. He had his trial by jury. He had smart lawyers. They did an excellent job, pleading to the court he he'd never been in any kind of legal trouble before. First offense. No record for drunk driving, or even a minor traffic accident. No speeding tickets. He was a good student, and a beloved member of his tennis club. Some outstanding parking tickets were there, maybe. That's all."

"Like everyone else."

"He was found guilty as charged." The corners of Hunter's eyes crinkled as he continued. "In California, the max penalty for a hit and run is four years behind bars. Vehicle code 20001 (a). The judge said he was obligated to follow the law as directed. However, he looked at Connery's background and clean record. A required treatment program was included in the sentence."

"Let me guess. Alan Connery was taken away, he did his four years and was released."

"Right. A treatment program required, and after four years he would be a free man. The woman he killed, Dorothy Hastings, was a nurse. An RN who worked at Community Hospital in San Luis Obispo. She'd bought coffee at a minimart and was crossing a main street, Santa Rosa, when she was hit and killed. Married, with two young kids, a girl about fourteen, a boy a few years younger. Dorothy Hasting's family attended the trial every single day. Husband, children, sister, and some in-laws. They weren't happy with the sentence."

"I think I've heard enough," Cora said.

"Just one more thing. There are newspaper files included here. Connery got off easy as far as the law was concerned. But he paid for it in other ways. Barred for life from professional tennis. NGOs hounded him, making him a poster boy against drunk driving. Seeing to it there were ongoing protest movements to pass stricter penalties. Several times he was assaulted on the streets in Los Angeles. He was ruined. Soon after, he disappeared from sight. No one knew where he went. His mother died a few years later. Grief can do that. His family never recovered, either. Sister's current name or whereabouts unknown. Father left the state, retired somewhere. Until that fight in Seattle some fifteen years later when he was finally recognized after his arrest."

"Alan Connery became a broken man," she whispered.

"Yes. By the time they picked him up in Seattle he was already considered a vagrant. Job to job. A transient lowlife. A drunk."

"All because of one dumb night's fun. So that's our unknown homeless man, huh? There are no doubts?"

"DNA doesn't lie, Cora."

"Do you think anyone around here remembers this crime?"

Hunter seemed preoccupied. "Here? Not likely. Happened a long time ago, across the country."

"You remembered it, Hunter."

He put a hand to his chin and wondered what she was getting at.

"I remembered when it was brought up. What are you alluding to?"

"Father Marcel. A few of the things he said. His love for tennis, even saying he played and would have tried turning pro, if not for his handicap. How old would Alan Connery be now?"

"Mid-fifties."

"About the same age as Father Marcel?"

"What are you getting at?"

"Maybe nothing. I'm not sure—yet."

Detective Hunter was impressed. "I get paid for investigating, Cora. I know you like to dabble in helping people, but this time it might be more than you can manage. Whoever went after our homeless man is dangerous. Extremely dangerous."

He added emphasis to his last words.

"Thanks for the warning. I'll keep that in mind."

"Keep me in the loop."

"Without a doubt. If not for your help, especially today, I'd be stuck at square one." She stood up. "And thanks for the coffee."

He held her arm, looked straight into her eyes. "Be careful, Cora. I mean it."

"I will. And I'll be in touch."

Cora did not immediately return to the diner. She checked in with Eddie Coltrane making sure everything was running well, then walked down the boulevard to the small park nestled behind St. Joseph's church. The weather was mild, trees were in full bloom. She slung her small bag over her shoulder and held her folded jacket over her arm. When she reached the park, she sat on one of the benches near the path leading to the steps of the church. For a while she closed her eyes, deep in thought, enjoying the late morning sunshine. The noise of a few laughing children caught her attention. Two women with strollers walked on by, nodding in her direction. She nodded back. Alan Mitchell Connery had killed a woman much like one of these mothers. And because of it, changed the course of Dorothy Hasting's family forever. All of her family paid a price. Like a rock thrown into water. A splash, and then endless ripples spreading further beyond. Cause and effect.

How would Alan Connery have reacted? No so much back then, when on trial, frightened and facing prison, but afterwards. During the long solitary nights when deeds are relived over and over. Would he feel the endless guilt of taking a life the way she had been forced to face regarding her own crime? Did he lose himself in drugs and alcohol, and ruin whatever life he might have salvaged? A wanderer, a transient without a home. Had this drunk driver really become a homeless vagrant who sat on the corner smelling of booze, ignored or given dirty looks, but also getting up to help schoolchildren cross at the light? A semi-famous rising star athlete, the entire world in his grasp, now a broken, isolated, and unreachable shell. Antisocial. Was there ever a realization, a moment of panic? Drinking to forget, to end the nightmare. Someone like that must despise himself, she thought. No forgiveness allowed.

Cora speculated about these possibilities, trying to see where puzzle pieces fit, and where they did not.

She walked toward the church, hoping the friendly priest could be found. She entered. It took time for her eyes to adjust to the dimness. Beside the altar she could see Father Marcel and several workmen lifting some boxes and taking them to the exit leading downstairs.

The priest noticed her walking down an aisle and came over to greet her. "Mrs. Gus, how nice to see you. How can I help?"

"When you have time, Father, I'd like us to have another private talk."

He wiped dirty hands on his jeans. "Right now, a couple of parishioners are helping me load some foodstuffs into the freezer downstairs. We're getting ready for the next community dinner in ten days." His mind was preoccupied with a long list of things needing to be done. "You would be a more than welcome volunteer or guest at our dinner. Your choice."

"You know I run a restaurant myself. If you'd like, come over to the Athena Diner. I bet my staff and I could give you lots of good suggestions in making food look appetizing. Keeping your customers satisfied."

"That's definitely an offer I'll gladly take you up on. Tell you what. Remember my little office over there?" He pointed to the door. "I'll probably be busy for about an hour, but if you'd like to stay, I have a pot of coffee waiting. You're more than welcome to relax, look over some of my piles of books. Do you like anthropology? There are a couple of new ones on my desk. Great new controversial discoveries on what happened to the Neanderthals."

"I'm fonder of dinosaurs."

"In that case," he retorted with a widened grin. "you could take a seat in one of the pews. Meditate, contemplate, or even pray. You might find it helps." Can he read me so easily, Cora wondered? Does this clever priest see through my armor and perceive my torment and sorrow?

"I think I might wait here. Thank you. Take your time, Father. And be careful with all those boxes. Don't hurt your back."

He laughed and returned to his waiting friends.

Cora took a seat in the sanctuary. Catholic churches had much in common with Greek Orthodox churches, yet also were so different, she mused. In the past two decades she hadn't attended a single religious service. Had anything changed? If taking a life was still a sin, even the life of a poisonous human snake, she still stood guilty. And if God's punishment was undeniable, was His wrath worse than the punishment she inflicted on herself?

"I'm ready to talk any time you are."

She opened her eyes to see Father Marcel looking at her.

"Were you meditating?"

"I was. I think I dozed off."

With a cheery smile he said, "I do that often. Follow me to my office. I'll make us both some fresh coffee, then we can chat."

"Sounds good."

His small office was as cluttered with papers and books as she remembered. She took a seat on the opposite side of the desk while her host poured two steaming mugs of coffee. "Maybe not as good as the Athena," he said offering her one. She thanked him as he reached atop the desk for his inhaler. "Excuse me. I need to use this. My throat is bothering me. Breath gets short."

He then sat down on his side and held the hot coffee waiting for it to cool. "So, things good? Going well, getting any answers for your investigation?"

"You were away a few days, weren't you?"

"Yep. I said I would be. No big trips unfortunately. In fact, I haven't had a real vacation since before this Covid horror began."

"I hear you. Luckily for me, business has been back to normal except for the odd new outbreak." She noticed several diplomas on the side wall, slightly askew. "I've been meaning to ask you. Last time you mentioned something about getting your divinity degree in California."

"I did, yes. Santa Clara University, Berkeley campus."

"Ah, the Bay Area. Nice."

"Lovely. You couldn't pick a better place to go to college. In fact, all these Berkeley types made me feel pretty dumb." He laughed as he sipped at the edge of his mug. A little coffee spilled, and he quickly wiped it up with a tissue. "Jesuits strongly believe in social justice and so do I. It made a perfect match." He seemed amused.

He was a very likable guy, Cora saw, impressive in many respects. She sipped from her own mug.

"So how did you wind up in New York? You must still miss the great weather out there. No snow."

"Well, remember I grew up in Montreal. Wintry weather here is nothing compared to Quebec, believe me. So, after I received my divinity credentials, I didn't hesitate to be assigned to a Jesuit diocese in the Bronx. A tough, poor neighborhood that needed all the help it could get. I enjoyed the work, especially with youngsters. Things happen. A few years later a few brothers were reassigned and retired from this diocese, and I was offered a place here. My superior wasn't well and someone higher up," he raised his eyebrows and looked up jokingly hinting at heaven, "and I found myself officially transferred on a permanent basis to St. Joseph's. Again, chance and luck."

"I for one are glad you're here," Cora quickly added. "I hope we can become friends."

"We can, Mrs. Gus. But tell me, it isn't curiosity about my school background that brought you here. How can I be of help?" He shifted a stack of books that blocked a direct view. Cora noticed an open pack of playing cards on the desk.

She leaned back and crossed her legs, mug still in hand. "Actually, I have some news I wanted to share with you in person."

"I hope it's good news," he said. "I could use some these days."

"Detective Hunter gets the credit for this. By utilizing a sample from a blood slide the hospital had in storage. It's routine looking for HIV or infectious diseases. Fortunately, he was able to have it retrieved before being discarded. Detective Hunter had it run through various national agencies seeking a match. It didn't take long until he hit one."

"Really? A stroke of luck for sure. You made an accurate match? You know his real name?"

She nodded. "I do. There is a criminal record for our friend 'Mitch.'"

"Well, I'm certainly glad you're getting closer. What's the name?"

She took a piece of paper from her purse and looked it over slowly. She purposely took her time. "Real name is Alan. Alan Mitchell Connery."

Hie eyes widened, and Father Marcel exhaled with pursed lips.

"That name mean something to you?"

"I may have heard it, as a matter of fact."

"He comes from California, age in the mid-fifties. It was a hit and run accident that happened more than thirty years ago. A woman was killed at a crosswalk. The victim's name was Dorothy Hastings. She was a nurse on her way to work an overnight shift."

"Sounds dreadful. Poor woman, poor family."

Cora listened and studied her companion's face. She thought the priest had been rather evasive the first time they spoke, and she didn't want to have that happen now. She decided to plead her cause openly and honestly.

"Can you give me some details to help jog my memory?" he said.

"The driver, Alan Connery, was leaving a beach town called Morro Bay. He was on his way to some important meeting scheduled early the next morning in Monterey, a few hours north. He was drunk and high. When the cops found his car the next morning he was asleep at a cheap motel. His blood level was still twice over the alcohol limit."

Father Marcel met her gaze with dismay.

"Here's my problem, Father. A few days back a worried woman I know begs me to help get information. We've all seen this homeless guy around. And it truly is awful what happened to him. I wonder, did he owe some dealer money for drugs? Or maybe he'd stolen some drugs? Maybe neither. Maybe it was a random act by some odious gangbanger out for kicks."

"We may never know the answer."

"I agree. So many possible reasons. Right now, I'm trying to learn who and why. Thing is," and here she placed her arms on the desk and looked straight at the priest, "everywhere I go no one wants to help. This baseball kid, Ramon, he played ball with our homeless guy and learned helpful tips. He knew nothing about the incident, but he did know where the guy was being cared for. Apparently, a janitor named Javier found him in an alleyway and brought him into his own house for several days. His wife bathed him, fed him, washed his wounds. They took real care, but then this guest suddenly gets up and leaves. He tells them he can't stay and had another place to go. But they knew nothing about where. Not even a name, where he went, or who might want to help. It's like banging into a brick wall of silence. Do you know this Javier? Is he a parishioner at St. Joseph's?"

"We do have several men in my community named Javier. I don't know if this janitor is one of them or not, but I can ask if you like. People resent it if we're too nosey."

"Listen, I'm not here to cause problems, Father. I just need to find him. Locate Alan Connery, try to learn who did this, and make sure they'll never be able to harm him again. I don't care about legalities or arrests. That's for the cops and the courts. My role is to see that he can live his life any way he wants. It's not for me to judge him." She met his gaze evenly.

"I hear you and understand your frustration," he said, aware the highly praised restaurant owner was a savvy, cultured, sophisticated woman. It was obvious she possessed a sharp mind and an ability to look beneath the surface. Admirable qualities to his way of thinking. Strong-willed, tireless in seeking answers and getting results.

"Please, Father," she continued. "Help me out as much as you can. I imagine you know more than you're willing to tell. And I respect that. Just keep in mind we're dealing with an intent to kill. To take a life. Isn't that something we hold sacred?"

Oh yes, she was sharp. "All life is sacred. But I need your promise, Mrs. Gus. Your word what I tell you remains between us. Can I be assured of it?"

"Yes Father, with the exception of criminal activity. Is that something you can live with? Do we have a deal?"

"We do. One more thing. You're aware I can't discuss anything that might have been told during confession. That's also sacred, my oath and obligation."

"Fair enough." The rules of engagement were set. "I think you know a lot more about Alan Mitchell Connery that you're willing to talk about."

Taken briefly aback, he said, "What makes you think that?"

"Honestly? A few things you talked about last time. Mostly tennis. About hoping to turn pro, playing in a few tournaments, and proving yourself to be a skilled athlete, at least until your asthma flared. That was a bad break. Your only choice was dropping out and surrendering your own ambitions. Dreams like that die hard, I know. And I feel sorry you never had the chance to fulfill your fantasy. The timing, though. You're the same age, and it occurred to me you might have met Alan Connery at some point. Maybe more than once. You two were playing in California simultaneously, and likely had similar matches."

He stared at her. Mrs. Gus was incredibly perceptive. "If you wanted to impress me, you have. Your deduction was correct. I loved the game. Back then it certainly was my life's goal. The reason I left Canada after high school was to go to California. Not for Hollywood or that kind of thing. I'd had tennis coaching back home, but Montreal isn't a town about that. And ice hockey isn't my style. My heart knew where I needed to be. Where the real game was, where the money was. I mean big money. Players, coaches, lifestyle. Women too. Professional sports are a small world, whatever league you play in. Pro tennis was growing rapidly. Excited crowds getting bigger every year. I saw potential for a poor boy from the grimy slums of Montreal."

"I assume you took advantage of your opportunity," Cora said with a little smirk.

"Every which way I could. After showing off my playing I was soon able to join USTA, the United States Tennis Association Southern California. They claim to produce champions and fill the stands. A uniquely polished group with access to world-class coaches, even then. Their world-class players included Billie Jean King. Pete Sampras…"

Cora whistled. "Impressive."

"They are serious people. Hard workouts, harder play, and often hard living off the court. The game is more than just serving and hitting a ball. Footwork, sideways, crossover. I learned so much. Needless to say, I met lots of hungry, ambitious people, that's part of the circuit. I even played a few minor matches in famous events. My name wasn't well known, but I bet you can probably still find me on the roster. Look up Marcel Legrand. That's my given name. I was popular in my performance class, but certainly didn't compete with the premium players."

"But from the reliable information I found, Alan Connery was among the best?"

"Alan…Yes. A rising star. It was written all over him. Good schools, top coaches, expert training since he was a young boy. When he was playing it was like watching ballet. Smooth moves, like music. He glided across the court. That boy had the best overhand and swing style I'd ever seen. L.A. newspapers did a couple of nice writeups about him. A future king of the court, headlines read. Alan was one year younger than me. I played against him a couple of time for fun. I don't need to tell you final scores. We'd never played a real match. I'd be too embarrassed." He paused. He seemed both wistful and lost in affectionate memory.

"Sounds like you really admired him."

"I did. It was hard not to. He may have been a golden boy on the clay court, but he wasn't arrogant. I'd call him a class act. Not someone scream-ing, hey look at me, I'm a winner. I never saw him argue when a chair umpire call went against him. Or get upset on the occasional loss. For all the obvious adoration and budding fame, I remember him as a guy standing on solid ground. Down to earth. Humble."

"Things must have changed eventually, though."

"Well, partying and drinking took a toll for sure. Maybe some drugs, but I never thought of him as becoming addicted to anything but tennis. Just having fun with his friends and fans."

"Tell me Father, were you aware of that fatal night?"

Father Marcel bit at his lower lip, remembering. "Where are you going with this?"

"To understand the circumstances. To learn the truth. Listen, Father, in my opinion what happened that night on a street corner wasn't a guy just getting beat up."

"What do you think it was?"

"I think it was attempted murder. The killer wanted him dead in a painful and brutal way."

Father Marcel sat contemplating something invisible. He drank his cooling coffee and avoided showing any emotion. "You may have a point," was all he said.

"Father, are you still holding back on me? Is there more to the story? More that you know about, I mean?"

"Let's say it's complicated. What happened here the other week isn't about his usual life in California."

Without saying so, he clearly did know more about the events of thirty plus years before. "Then you did know about the hit and run?" she asked gently, not trying to prod the priest into telling things that made him uncomfortable.

He nodded. She rested her hands on her lap. "Then I assume you were living in California the night of the tragedy?"

"The night it happened I was in Morro Bay."

A cold shiver ran down Cora's back. This news was something she was not expecting. "Are you telling me you were there, with Alan that night?"

"I wasn't *with* Alan. However, I was at that beach party. Maybe a hundred people showed up. Some girls from Santa Monica had rented a beach house for a week. The town is a good place for surfing, and San Luis Obispo is also wine country. It draws tons of people. Not only tourists. Southern California types like the Central Coast. Not as crowded, beautiful beaches, good places to eat, moderate prices compared to Santa Barbara." He looked awkward, not certain what to say next. "I quit smoking years ago," he muttered. "Right now, I wish I had a cigarette."

"I'd be happy to give you one. But it's bad for your asthma."

"True enough." He appeared to think carefully before continuing. "I drove up that morning with a few buddies from the club. Everyone was excited about the party. It was rumored a few celebs might be coming too. Naturally, Alan was going to be there. He'd bragged about a meeting in Monterey he was having the next day. A new contract. Some tennis bigshots were ready to sign him. Get him for upcoming tours. This was going to be his chance to show what he could do against the best. I don't know which players, but notable ones who drew the crowds. That's all that mattered. So, Alan was in a really good place and a really good mood. I don't recall if he got to the beach house before me or after. All I can tell you is that he was stoked. Imagine this kid, just past twenty, and being signed for prestigious tours like the ATP Challenger Tour. Play good ball now and he'd soon be on his way to the Grand Slams."

"I enjoy watching tennis myself. Finals in Italy. The French open, US Open. It is exciting. I loved watching on television growing up in Athens."

"Then you know. The excitement. The fever. A few other local players coaxed him to have some champagne to celebrate. They popped a few bottles. But they weren't happy when he popped a few pills and drank a few glasses of hard stuff. For the first time he wasn't showing discipline. He wasn't being professional. A couple of the girls also tried to stop him, pry him away to the beach or someplace. He'd have been better off having sex with them than continuing to party. But the excitement went to his head, and he let himself go. Sometime after midnight he made an effort to leave, to do the drive, up Freeway 101 to Monterey. I know I tried to stop him. Others too. He wasn't steady, and he knew it. 'I'm okay, I'm okay,' he kept insisting. He dunked his head, drank coffee, even vomited. He needed to be ready for the interview. Someone or other offered to drive him up there. It's about a hundred forty miles. He said no. He'd stop to sleep a bit, he insisted. He was fine. Leave him alone."

Father Marcel sighed deeply. "Then off he went. His car peeled out of the driveway and down the road. His friends were concerned. One even suggested calling the Highway Patrol to stop him. He'd get a big fat fine, of course, but he'd be kept safe. The road to the 101 Freeway from Morro Bay takes you straight into the center of San Luis Obispo. There are a couple of hospitals downtown, I recall. Looking for the highway is when he made some wrong turn and cut a light. That's when it happened."

Cora put a hand to her mouth. "He hit the nurse on her way to work."

"Yes. That split second mistake…It cost that poor woman her life and ruined his." The priest hung his head. Cora saw his anguish and felt pain of her own. What a needless horror. Two lives utterly destroyed. Plus the mourning family of the nurse, devastated as well.

They sat silently for a time, letting the effects of the catastrophe sink in. Instead of playing tournaments and being hailed in newspapers and adored by the public, Alan Mitchell Connery found himself sentenced to state prison. A hit and run conviction under the influence of alcohol. The jury found him guilty. Manslaughter.

"I felt sorry for him. I admit that. It wasn't for me to judge him. I went to visit him in prison. Several times."

"And how was he?"

The priest shook his head. "He was hurting. Wretched. I'd never seen anyone in such a state. He broke down and cried. None of his former friends ever visited. They kept far away, wanting nothing to do with him. And not wanting the association to rub off or taint them. He admitted he couldn't sleep. Haunted by nightmares. He was suffering over what he'd done, reliving that moment over and over. He wasn't looking forward to his release. He deserved this punishment and more. He said his life was over. This was not the happy-go-lucky man I'd admired. This was someone lost. Tortured. Troubled. A totally different person than the one I knew. By this time, I was already at the seminary. I told him of my plans to join the priesthood. Alan was raised Catholic, you know. He asked me to plead to God for mercy. It was heartbreaking to hear. A stupid mistake that happened in an instant. I gave him my word, reminding him about forgiveness. I visited him one more time, more than a year later. He remained a broken man. Looked much older than his age. The only hint of a smile I saw was when I told him I was graduating. That I would be a Jesuit helping lost souls in New York. I gave him my phone number. I asked him to keep in touch. He said he would, someday."

"And did he ever call you?"

"Yes, but rarely. On the road, never giving me any useful information. If I knew where he was, I could have contacted a local diocese to search for him. To give him support. It was useless. I prayed for him, and for Dorothy Hastings and her loved ones too. The whole incident was a Shakespearian tragedy."

"I'm so sorry," Cora whispered, thinking back of her own senseless act.

"Now you know everything I can tell you," Father Marcel said, his voice slow and sad.

"Where is he now, Father? Do you have any idea at all?"

"When we began this conversation," he reminded. "I gave my promise to tell you everything I could, outside of things told during confessional. There's nothing else I can say without breaking that vow. I have no choice in the matter."

"I do understand, Father. Thank you for all your help." She wiped a welling tear from the corner of her eye. Father Marcel acknowledged her with a handshake as she made to leave. "Do you think that the beating was more than random?" she asked. "Is Alan Connery still in danger?"

Without hesitation his answer was, "Yes."

15

HER CELL PHONE RANG. "ATHENA Diner, can I help you?"

"Hey Cora, it's me."

"Hunter? Got a little time? I need to talk."

"Funny you should say that. I'm taking a personal day off. A drive to the Queens Zoo? We can discuss things on the way. I can pick you up in about fifteen minutes."

Cora looked over at the clock centered above the cashier's station. Lunch hour was almost finished. The dining booths and tables were steadily emptying out. "Make it twenty. I have special instructions to give the kitchen staff regarding tonight's Greek specials."

She combed her hair, took her lightweight jacket off the hook and left. Hunter was sitting inside his dark SUV idling in front of a fire hydrant. He leaned over to push the door on the passenger side open, and she slid in easily. "Ready to go?" He asked,

She nodded. "Are you really taking us to the Queens Zoo?"

"Sure. It's the site of the old World's Fair back in 1964. You've seen all those postcards."

"I have indeed," she said with an amused laugh. "Good thing I brought along a jacket."

They drove to the nearby Grand Central Parkway through Flushing Meadows Park. "So, what's your news?" he asked, glancing her way.

Cora fumbled through her bag for her sunglasses. It was a bright day, not quite as warm as it should be at this time of year. "I went to see Father Marcel. And we had a nice long talk. It turns out he did know the name of Alan Connery."

"So, your intuition was right."

"More than that. Turns out he knew our victim personally way back when."

"Wow." He was impressed. Somehow Cora's uncanny abilities at finding things out always fascinated him.

She explained in thorough detail the priest's encounters with their nameless victim both before the hit and run as well as after. Hunter was more than surprised to hear specifics of the intimate connection. "How would you like to proceed, boss?" he asked.

"I'm no cop, Jonah." She reminded. "Just someone who likes to ask lots of questions."

"Sly as a fox, too. Better than a regular cop like the rest of us. Honestly, I admire your tenacity. I try and look at crime scenes from all angles. Pieces of puzzles to fit together. You have this particular ability to hone right in."

"Smoke and mirrors. You're giving me too much credit. I go with my feelings. My gut. Experience in life has taught me that the hard way."

They took the exit two stops before the signs announcing LaGuardia International Airport and made their way to the entrance for the Queens Zoo.

It took a while until they came to the parking area, and had to search before they could find a parking space situated not too far from the aviary. The renowned huge dome was easy to recognize, and open year-round.

"You like birds, Mrs. Gus?"

"Cora, I told you to call me Cora. And yes, I love birds."

They left the car and entered through the wide gates. "This aviary is super famous for its variety of hundreds of varied species." Hunter noted.

Several school children's classes were busy taking tours inside, and Hunter and Cora followed closely behind one of them.

"This is a everybody's favorite," the informative tour guide was saying, pointing her hand toward a particular breed. "She's a Scarlet Macaw. A member of the parrot family." The red and yellow bird was standing on a bar, staring down as intently at the schoolchildren as the kids were staring at it. It was a magnificent creature. With long wings colored first red, then yellow toward the middle, and blue all the way down. As if showing off, the bird flapped it long wings, raised them wide, and flew to the highest point of the dome. Then she plunged like a dive bomber.

Hunter's jaw gaped. "Look at that!"

Cora poked him in the ribs. "You know you're like a kid yourself," she said.

"Only when I'm off duty. Besides, I don't get many chances to put the ugliness of the real world behind."

The macaw circled, then landed back at the same bar on the same spot. Behind it, as if not to be outdone, an American Eagle and a big white cattle egret put on a similar show. There were hundreds of birds in the aviary. A collection of species found across the Americas.

A great horned owl seemed to be eyeing them as they moved on. "I've been tinkering with an idea on what to do next," she said when they stopped again.

"I bet you are. Are you aware of how many people talk about you helping them, especially with things that I'd consider to be crimes? It really is very complimentary. When did you start to be an investigator?"

"You think I'm a private detective? Like on television?" she giggled at that. Feeling schoolgirlish herself, and almost like she was out on a date with Detective Hunter.

"No, really. You've earned quite a reputation in the community, don't you know that? And I must admit in this matter you've impressed me. Did you have any police background in your family back in Athens?"

"*My* family?" She laughed out loud. "Heavens, no. My father was a tough, hard-nosed businessman. No nonsense. Import and export. The main function of the police was to be bribed."

He raised his dark brows. "I see."

"It's not like that anymore. In a way, investigating things that weren't my business did begin back in Greece. After university I was hired by the American Embassy. Mostly for translation, but I was promoted fairly soon. Languages were my specialty. I studied both English and Russian. Literature, too. My Russian was good, but I excelled in English. So, having someone available in Athens who could work on all three, written documents as well real time conversation was an asset."

He whistled. "Most English speakers know only one language. You excelled at three. Tough ones, too."

"The Ambassador back then, Mary Overstreet, took a liking to me. I was a hard, good worker. Are you familiar with her?"

"Overstreet? Never heard it before."

"She stationed me in a separate area where many of the documents I worked on were decidedly classified at different levels. My duties became more and more involved with some of their top people from D.C."

"Ah. The spies we sent you."

That comment hit a nerve, and she struggled not to show emotion. "Well, when you work in a foreign country, I guess you could call everyone a spy of some sort. I did learn a lot, though. It wasn't hard for me to discover during a conversation I was translating when one of the talkers was being honest or lying. You learn how to read facial expressions and the like. When people look down or avert their eyes. When they laugh too much, or when they never smile. You deduce from these type of things. Next you report your observations to your supervisors. Evidently, I did the job well. I really did work with some of the best."

"I don't mean to snoop, but am I right that you were once engaged to someone from the embassy? That's what a few of the precinct cops heard at the diner from gossipy employees."

She stopped and regarded Hunter. "Yes. That was more than twenty years ago. His name was Dirk Bonneau. He died. He was killed. His car was blown up by terrorists."

Hunter covered his eyes with a hand. "Oh God, Cora. I didn't mean to rake up past wounds. Please, please forgive me."

"It's all right. As I said, all that happened many, many years ago. After an emotional meltdown I managed to pick myself up. I had no idea where my life was heading at the time. My family had a few distant relatives in America, so my parents urged me to fly over for a while, see if I liked it here, and try to begin a new life."

"Did you like America?"

"Yes, very much. But life here was complicated. However, this is where I met Gus Padnos, as you know. He gave me a place to stay with his sister, and a job to earn a little money. Gus was a good man. He offered me that new life I needed, and that paved the way to try to forget the past. I owed Gus so much. We married a year after I started work at the Athena. I knew he already suffered some medical issues. We were together almost ten years when, unfortunately, his heart gave out. Gus fought his illness like a champion, never letting it break him. He was satisfied with his life. His pride and joy was what he created, The Athena Diner. It became the child he never had. I still visit his elderly sister whenever I can. She was an immense help to me also. I think all of this happened before you arrived at the precinct."

Cora then turned the tables. "And what's your story, Detective?"

"My dad was on the force. He became a captain a few years before he retired. I also have two cousins who are cops, so you could say it's in my blood. I was studying at John Jay College of Criminal Justice. During our years of fighting terrorism overseas, like lots of guys I decided to sign up, finish my degree after. The army sent my unit to Afghanistan, and I came home in bad shape. I lost a couple of close friends there. And I saw so much cruelty on both sides. Needless suffering. All for nothing. It was sickening. After returning stateside they diagnosed me with PTSD. I had these flashbacks, vivid memories of events, nightmares. I felt emotionally cut off from people."

When he spoke about trauma it struck Cora how much she and Hunter had shared in their pasts.

"The V.A. gave me good care, a good therapist too. They put me into group therapy with other vets. It helped. I was more fortunate than most, finishing my degree, getting hired by NYPD and starting a good career. I married my longtime girlfriend, and we had two kids. A girl and a boy. But the marriage didn't last. I take the blame. I still had too many scars. Anger, always jumpy, trouble concentrating. Too much for Angie to deal with." He smiled thinly. "So now I see my kids every other weekend. I pick them up, they stay with me, I drive them back to their mom on Long Island."

"I'm sorry for your pain, Hunter. At least you know where you stand."

"Well, it's a little more complicated than that."

"Please. I'd like to hear."

"My ex-wife remarried. I don't mind, good luck to them. The husband, however, has this notion of moving down to Florida. He claims he has some business opportunity. Fine again. The problem is that he has a lawyer, his brother, who keeps filing these nuisance motions meant to pressure me into giving up my parental rights giving them freedom to move. But if my kids live that far away, I won't get to see them at all."

"Sounds like a mess."

"Yeah, it is. Sorry, Cora. I don't mean to dump all this on you. I think I just need a friend." Hunter stopped, frowned.

"It sounds unfair, " Cora said.

"Thanks for listening. Believe me, it helps to talk." He glanced up at a fast-moving cloud. "So, there you have Jonah Hunter's life in a nutshell."

"Well, I'm on your side. I know a few good lawyers."

He grinned. "And I may need one. Listen. Let's change the mood. How about we get some ice cream? There's a stand across the way."

"Sounds good. For now, we can get back to this business."

They bought French vanilla cones, licking them as they toured the zoo. While watching Texas Longhorns feed, Cora said, "I have another theory regarding who may have tried to kill Alan Connery."

Hunter's tongue lapped up a large drip that was about to spill off the cone. "Hmm. I'm not surprised. Tell me about it." Coyotes prowled among bushes nearby. She spoke thoughtfully, slowly, fitting together pieces like the crossword puzzles Hunter liked to solve. When she felt she had most of the elements resolved, she said, "I'm going to need your help again. And this time it could be dangerous."

"That's why I carry a gun."

They continued along random paths finishing their ice cream. From a distance the two of them looked like a couple of college kids.

The daylight was beginning to fade. They made a few more brief stops to watch bison chewing their cuds and view Canadian lynxes dart into the shadows. It was growing late, and Cora needed to return to the diner for the expected busy dinner rush.

They made their way back to the parking lot. As Hunter sat behind the wheel and started the car, Cora added, "After we discuss a few more ideas I have, there are a couple of phone calls I need to make."

16

"LILLIAN?"

"Yes. Is that you, Mrs. Gus?"

"Hi. Yes. I've been wanting to call you." She paused. "A little good news. The homeless man you talked about. He's been located." She could all but feel the sense of excitement on the other end.

"Wonderful! I'm so glad to hear it. What else can you tell me?"

"It's so busy here at work. I can't talk now. Just wanted you to know. It looks like he's healing and doing better. I was told he's been seen on a bench at the little park behind St Joseph's. Know it?"

"Yes. Of course, I do."

"Good. Then if you like try going over. Maybe he'll be there this evening or late tonight."

"That's wonderful to hear, Mrs. Gus. I'll do that. I can't thank you enough. You're the best."

"No problem, Lillian. Listen, I gotta go. We'll talk more, I promise. See you soon." She hung up, put her cell back into her pocket and hurried to the kitchen where Chef Claude was speeding a backlog of dinner meals.

After making the rounds of the tables and booths, chatting briefly with customers old and new, Cora saw the sunlight had begun to pass below tall neighboring buildings. The Jamaica Avenue El train, with its brakes rattling, pulled into the nearby station. She needed to leave, and again asked

Eddie Coltrane to cover for her and to close if she hadn't returned in time. In the bathroom she put on jeans, a red hoodie over her blouse, and running sneakers. Then she left without normal goodbyes.

It was near the culmination of rush hour, cars searching local streets for scarce parking spaces. A uniformed officer from the nearby precinct waved and said hello as she darted across the street and headed towards the sun-glinted tall spire of St Joseph's in the distance.

As she hurried, she focused on her breathing, recalling the instructions her teacher had taught in yoga class. She paid attention to the rhythm of her breath, taking air in slowly and deeply, counting to five, then pushing it out slowly and calmly. Repeat again and again until you find the stillness you're seeking, she'd learned.

She could feel the rising and expanding in her stomach as she drew air in, and it falling as she let it out. It was a brisk, short walk to the church.

Dusk was fast approaching by the time she reached St. Joseph's. The church doors were closed shut, but she noticed lights turning on inside a few second story windows of the adjoining rectory. Opposite from where she was standing the old park behind the church was growing quiet. A few evening strollers walked in different directions along the winding path.

On either side of the asphalt walkway stood rows of tall aging trees and big shrubs of numerous types. The thick twisting branches, leaves, and tree trunks hid most lights beginning to glimmer on the wide boulevard only two blocks away. Above branches intertwined, forming a canopy over her head. Sounds of buses and cars in the distance remained muffled. She was startled when, without warning, a young man on a skateboard sped by. She turned towards the distant row of park benches now mostly unoccupied. Walking from the opposite direction a young couple were strolling with a floppy-eared brown and white beagle. A senior citizen arose from a bench, and with the aid of his cane carefully made his way toward the line of detached and semi-detached houses leading to the boulevard and its numerous tall apartment buildings.

A mild breeze produced rustlings amid the new foliage. Rays of dimming sunlight shone through the myriad gaps between the leaves and delivered rich hues of dappled light over the worn pavement. Cora leaned against the gnarled trunk of a wide maple, leaving her mostly in shadows but with a clear view of the nearby park benches.

She took off her sunglasses and made herself comfortable on the dry grass, sitting with her back against the tree's trunk. She placed her leather strapped shoulder bag beside her. She took out her phone and checked it. The signal was good, three bars, her battery almost full. She tuned into a soft music station and kept her eyes keenly on the asphalt path ahead. She had brought a sandwich to eat and placed it on her lap. She also took a bottle of water from her bag and drank a few sips. It was liable to be a long wait, she knew, and she hoped she would still have enough stamina to endure as long as necessary after today's unexpectedly busy workday at the diner. Nearby, a small squirrel sat observing her with a curious look. As she kneeled to reach out, it scampered away into a clump of bushes.

Cora pushed hair from her face. Waning sunlight was vanishing. A small dog ran off its leash, and right behind a young woman frantically dashed to catch it. Cora dug fingertips into the soft earth. It felt good, renewed. She could smell pine needles and nearby budding flowers. Being close to nature always made her feel refreshed and relaxed. She wished she had more time to spoil herself. She thought nostalgically of the trips to the villa she had taken with Dirk. The two of them amid the beauty of the countryside. How wonderful those days had been—She cut the memories short. That was then, this was now. She turned her attention back to the park. The sky was darkening rapidly now. She felt chilly when a stronger breeze blew by. She pulled up the hood over her head and returned her concentration back to the path and the benches.

A crying baby in a carriage being pushed by a harried mother appeared and grew smaller as the woman rushed to get home. Cora watched the woman and wondered how different her own life could have been if only… if only. Again, she cut the thoughts off.

As dark set in the streetlamps in the park turned on. She stood back up, away from the light but with an unobstructed view of the area. She put her phone away and held her stitched leather shoulder bag against her breast. Again, she practiced her breathing technique to remain calm. A few moments later she heard noises coming from behind. She turned to see a trio of teenagers cut across from the side of the church and cross the street at an angle from the park to the next street.

Time passed slowly and the blanket of night replaced remaining dim hues of sky. Lights from the boulevard were bright in the distance.

As she remained focused on the benches a solitary figure appeared in the distance. As he came closer, she could see he was wearing a baseball cap pulled low with the brim hiding his eyes. He wore an old jacket with the zipper open, a plaid workman's shirt untucked over worn jeans. He was carrying a paper bag, likely holding a can or bottle of beer. He looked around before he picked a place and sat on the corner of a wooden bench at the edge of the adjacent lamplight's glow. There was a small bandage on the side of his face. He pulled his legs in close to his stomach, and Cora could see he was wearing worn workman's shoes. Once he settled comfortably into his space, he lifted the bag and drank. Apart from shifting a bit to get more comfortable he seemed to relax. He placed the paper bag down next to him and rubbed his hands together. It was becoming chilly now that the sun was gone. He slouched slightly and crossed his legs, stifling a yawn, crossing his arms. She couldn't see if his eyes were open or closed.

The park was quiet and lonely save for traffic sounds from the boulevard. Behind her she could see buttery light emitting from the church rectory windows.

She glanced at her phone for the time. It was not yet late.

Someone was walking from the other direction. A long shadow appeared from the streetlamp nearer to her. A new figure appeared. He wore a dark hoodie pulled over his head. Dark blue or black, she couldn't tell. He seemed well built, not too tall. He was wearing white sneakers. Both hands were in his pockets. He was taking his time, glancing here and there, not in any rush. Cora made ready to move.

The new arrival passed her and walked closer to the man on the bench. He stopped in the middle of the path some feet away from the sitting man, standing at his full height.

"Alan Connery," he said in a strong baritone voice.

The figure on the bench raised his head and eyed him, not responding.

"I didn't finish what I began last time. Tonight, I will." He sneered as he spoke.

The man on the bench still said nothing.

A steady hand pulled from the pocket holding a sharp thin steel knife. The blade glinted in the light of the streetlamp. He held it steady, turning it menacingly this way and that. "You can stand up and face me, or you can twist on your bench. Don't matter to me." He raised his arm with the knife now held high.

Cora appeared from the grove of trees behind. "Put that knife down—now!"

The man spun around, a surprised stare on his face. Cora stood with her feet apart, shoulders back. Her hood was pulled down, A hank of hair fell over the left side of her face.

"Who the fuck are you?" he demanded.

"I'm you're worst fucking nightmare, Kyle."

"What?" he was shocked at the use of the name. "You know me?" He looked ready to point the tip of the sinister shiny blade at her.

Before he could refocus, she lifted both hands up, a pistol aimed straight for his belly. "Drop the knife. Do it."

He hesitated for a fleeting moment, then complied. The knife clanked to the ground.

"Now move away, slowly."

Any sign of cockiness evaporated. He became unsettled. "I didn't hurt anyone. Why are you pointing that at me?"

"Because you intended to kill that man on the bench, Kyle."

Kyle was perplexed. "How do you know my name?"

"I know lots about you, Kyle Hastings. You're the son of Dorothy Hastings. The victim of a senseless hit and run more than thirty years ago."

He was stunned, not knowing what to say. His lips were trembling, brows furrowed.

Cora held her gaze and her gun firmly. "That man isn't your concern."

"Do you know who that is over there? *He's* a callous murderer, not me." He voice became impassioned. "He *killed* my mother. Drunk, and drove away. He left her to die in the street. My dad's life was wrecked too, and mine was nearly ruined as well."

"But now you have a family of your own to care about. Kick the knife away from you."

He did as told as quickly as he could.

"That's fine. Step under the streetlamp." Cora lowered her gun but remained ready to use it. "I know the entire story, Kyle. It was tragic for everyone. More than thirty years have passed since then, and that man on the bench has paid for his crime. He was in prison."

"And released after four years," he said with contempt. "*Four years.* Do you call that punishment for a life stolen? He's a butcher. A lowlife druggie thug. I finally found him, and I won't apologize for it."

"You don't have to. But when you attacked him with that bat it was attempted murder. And if you succeeded with that knife tonight, it would officially become homicide. And now you'd become that killer. That bully who beat on a homeless man."

Beads of sweat appeared on his brow, and he wiped them away with his sleeve. "He deserves that and more. For years I've dreamed of finding that bastard someday." He stabbed a finger toward the bench. "That rich boy, the famous tennis player, so full of himself."

"Revenge is a gift that keep on giving, huh? Take a hard look at yourself, Kyle," she said bluntly. "Alan Connery has paid a heavier price than you or me could imagine. Your mother's tragedy was his too. It wrecked his career and kept him haunted with guilt every step of the way, year after year for his whole life. He was never the same. He became a drifter, hired and fired from job to job. With no life, no family, no home. A man riddled with self-loathing and blame, his own punishment worse than anything the penal system could deliver. He passed sentenced on himself to be tormented, to drink into infinite oblivion—a slow death. He didn't care, he just wanted his pain to stop. Thirty plus years of self-inflicted damage. Think about it. The man you hate so much isn't even a shadow of his former self. No prison cell could succeed in giving such a sentence of such torture."

A single tear fell down Kyle's face. "Now I'm somehow supposed to feel pity for him?" He glanced over his shoulder. The man on the bench remained unmoving. "You won again, didn't you?" He told him with pursed lips.

At that, the man raised himself up, reached inside his pocket and pulled out a gold badge and showed it in the light. "NYPD," was all he said. Kyle's eyes grew wide, startled as the cop unhooked a set of handcuffs from his belt.

"How did you find me? How did you know?"

"When you appear in court you can ask your lawyer."

"This must be some kind of set-up." He was growing frantic.

"No set-up," said Cora, her voice softening as she moved more toward Kyle. "This was about preventing you from committing murder tonight. Or would you prefer to become the one in prison? You have a wife and family of your own back home, I've been told. A couple of kids."

"Two. We have a boy and a girl."

"You live in Los Angeles, Westwood. A nice place. You and a partner run a commercial insurance business. Your wife's name is Beth. She teaches school, doesn't she? See, I know all I need to."

The facts of his background threw him. His head tilted, features contorted. How did she know all this, how could anyone know? He stammered, but no audible words were forthcoming.

"You knew exactly what you were doing by coming here tonight. But it didn't pay off. Bad choice."

Hunter spoke for the first time. "But we all make our choices in life," he said, no longer looking like the vulnerable figure hunching on the bench. He pulled off the bandage from the side of his face, standing upright and menacing.

"This is entrapment," Kyle mumbled.

"Oh? Well, we can discuss it at Central Booking."

"What do you mean? Am I under arrest?" He gazed at the dangling handcuffs and began to panic.

"Being arrested could be your decision," retorted Cora in a tranquil tone.

Kyle turned back to face her again. His shoulders sagged; he swallowed several times. He became a shell of the threatening attacker filled with bravado scarcely a few minutes earlier.

"You can be arrested right now and booked. Sure, a pricy lawyer might get you a good plea deal. You carried a bat last time. When you went after Alan Connery, the court considers a bat to be a lethal weapon. If you're very lucky maybe you get away with aggravated assault instead of attempted murder. Whatever sentence even a lenient judge might pronounce will still haul your ass upstate to maximum security. You've heard of Attica? Now it will be *your* family that's been ruined. Your future, your life, your kids growing up without their dad. And even worse, if you did kill him, you'll become no different than him."

Kyle got it. He had a flash of his kids without a dad, his wife branded by tonight's act. He realized he was caught in a trap. He was scared.

"Or," said Cora abruptly, "you could walk away a free man. Leave right now, walk straight to the boulevard, take a taxi to JFK International. Catch that redeye midnight flight to Los Angeles."

"You'd let me do that?'

"If I do, you'll speak with *nobody* about this, call *nobody*. Not even stopping for your bags. Got it? You'll erase this whole episode as though it never happened. And you'll never come back to this area of New York."

He nodded definitively.

She paused, then raised her voice and changed tone. "One more thing. If ever you try to bring harm to Alan Connery, we'll come looking for you. In fact, if *anyone* brings harm to Alan Connery, you'll see us in California. We found you this time and we will again. Don't doubt it for a second. So, now it's in your own interest to keep him safe, understand what I'm telling you, Mister Hastings? Yes?" She tapped an impatient foot waiting for an answer.

"You'll really let me go?" he asked dubiously. "After what happened, after that fight we were in?"

"Was that a fight, you say? Okay. Let's call it a fight between a homeless drunk and a misguided fool. Sounds like two losers to me."

Kyle didn't budge. He looked to Hunter and back to Cora with narrowed eyes. It was difficult to imagine they were actually offering him a way out.

"Agreed or not, Kyle?" asked Hunter.

"Agreed," Kyle blurted, still confused and disoriented by the precipitous turn of events. His world had turned upside down, become surreal, but he realized he might actually have a way out.

Hunter picked up the knife and carefully placed it in the paper bag with his bottle of lemon and lime soda.

"Let's say you managed to escape our custody and leave it at that, Kyle. Do you hear me?"

Kyle nodded again. "I hear you loud and clear."

Cora pointed a finger toward the city lights. "The boulevard is right over there. Move. Get the hell out of here, now."

Kyle turned to leave, unsure if they planned to shoot him in the back or actually release him. Edging his way shakily, he began his slow walk but soon picked up speed and continued at a brisk pace that didn't stop. Cora and Hunter eyed him as he gradually disappeared in the dark.

Hunter exhaled. It had been a good night's work. They glanced at each other with a small smile of success.

"You're a real badass, Cora." He commended her, tucking in his shirt, fastening the handcuffs back onto his belt. "You managed him like a pro. By the way, I checked you out to be sure your gun is licensed."

"Of course, it's licensed. I run a busy business that deals with a lot of cash. The city gave me a legitimate permit." She placed the gun carefully inside a holster in her bag.

"You scared him half to death with that weapon. You looked like you really know how to use it."

"I took a lesson once," she replied with a frown.

"One more question. What if Kyle hadn't put down that knife when you told him to? If he'd held onto it, turned on you, would you have shot him?"

She looked straight at Hunter. "What do you think?"

He wondered what she might have done but couldn't decide. Tonight, he saw an aspect of the Athena Diner owner he hadn't encountered before. If he had to bet, though, his money would say she would have used the gun without flinching.

"By the way, Detective, I haven't thanked you for your assistance tonight. You did great, also. I owe you big time."

"You're not finished with this untidy business yet. Good luck with the rest. Be careful, Cora. You can thank me later."

"I will." She took out her phone. "I'll speak with you tomorrow. Hopefully, by then everything in this matter will be resolved. One way or another."

Hunter nodded. He came over and hugged her gently. For a brief moment their eyes met and locked.

"Keep safe, Mrs. Gus." He said softly.

"Cora. I told you, call me Cora. We're not at the restaurant."

He laughed and waved as he turned to walk toward his parked car.

She drew a deep breath and made her first call. It was to Lillian Gorman. "Lillian? Hi. This is Mrs. Gus. From the diner."

"Oh hello, Mrs. Gus. So nice to hear your voice. I've been wondering when you'd call. Do you have any news for me?"

"Listen, I do have news. I'm busy and can't talk now, but if you'll come to the diner tomorrow morning, I think I'll have some answers you'll want to hear."

"Good news, I hope! Thank you. I'll look for you in the morning. Goodnight."

Cora hung up and looked toward the church rectory. The lights were on. She quickly made her final call for the night.

"Hello, Father Marcel. I told you I'd let you know when things were done. They are, I promise. Listen, I'm very close to the rectory, and if it's not too late I'd like to come by now."

"It's not too late. Come over. I'll be waiting at the rectory door."

17

SHE KNOCKED ON THE HEAVY wooden door. It opened wide. Father Marcel stood and greeted her. "Good evening, Father."

He took her hand. "I'm glad you came. Come on in."

She looked up the flight of stairs. A door on the right was slightly ajar. "May I go up?" she asked.

"Yes, you may."

"Alone?"

He acquiesced immediately. "Yes, alone. But first, if you don't mind, I do have one question."

"Ask away. After tonight anything goes."

He thought for a moment. "How did you know that Alan Connery was here in the rectory?"

She made a face. "Well, Father, you sort of told me yourself."

"I did?"

"When we were talking the other night in your office. Remember there was a stack of books blocking our view of each other? You pushed them to the side so we could see more easily."

"I remember. What about it?"

"There was an open deck of playing cards I noticed on the desk. So, I thought to myself, either Father Marcel sure likes to play solitaire, or maybe he's been playing cards with someone."

"And how did you know I wasn't playing cards with Father Jerome, my junior assistant?"

"I didn't." She regarded him with a girlish grin. "Call it a hunch. And you confirmed it when I called you. I deduced you were more protective of Alan Connery than you were willing to admit. The way you spoke, it wasn't about giving a homeless man a meal. It wasn't even about obligations from hearing his confession. No, sorry. It was regarding you being there for a friend. A friend you never stopped caring about. It says a lot about you as a person, Father. The man, not the priest."

This caught the churchman by surprise.

"You're not only quick, but you're wise."

She laughed at his remark. If only he knew.

"No one can blame you for keeping his whereabouts a secret," she said. "I go to casinos sometimes. I'm not a big gambler but I like to play. I look at the odds. Poker, blackjack. Roulette. So here it was like adding two plus two. Alan was an acquaintance from more than thirty years ago, you told me. All of a sudden, he became just another homeless guy to feed. I don't think so. There was more to it. I felt it. So, the odds were on my side. And it was simple to realize your rectory seemed a perfect place for recuperation. I took a shot in the dark. A big shot, I will admit."

"I see you really do like to take chances."

"It can become addictive." She winked and touched his arm. "It's been a long, difficult day for me, Father. Can you trust and allow me to go upstairs now, please? Alone?"

He considered and grinned. "Go ahead, Sherlock. You've earned it."

She walked through the unadorned hallway and walked up the stairs slowly, bag slung over her shoulder, hand holding onto the wooden banister. When she reached the landing, she waited to catch her breath. Then she knocked lightly at the partly open door. "May I come in?"

A voice said, "Yes."

She pulled the door fully open and stood beneath the frame. "Do you remember me?" she asked the man sitting in a straight-backed heavy wooden chair beside the window.

"I do. You're Mrs. Gus. The diner lady. You always give my coffee for free. And sometimes sandwiches too."

"Yes. And I'm glad to see you, Alan Mitchell Connery."

She came into the room and sat in a chair placed beside a small table with a lamp, an empty mug, and a bible.

He regarded her with vacant, sad eyes. An aura of melancholy impossible to miss radiated from him. His head had been shaved, and his hair was beginning to grow back. She saw a number of yellow and green healing bruises on his face and neck. One cheekbone was swollen, and there were scabs where stitches had been removed at the base of his skull. A bandage along the side of his right eye was discolored from dried blood. The eye was puffy and damaged, but it didn't seem his sight had been affected. He was wearing a clean white tee shirt, and she noticed defensive wounds on his arms. A cursory glance verified how he tried to protect himself from Kyle's blows. He was wearing a clean pair of slacks, sandals on his feet, and they also seemed slightly swollen.

"It looks like you're healing well," she said, struggling not to show her grieved feelings for him.

"I'm working on it." His voice was dry and staccato.

"Should I be calling you Mitch, now? Is that what you call yourself?"

"No one's used the name Alan for an awfully long time. Whenever anyone recognized me, it always meant more trouble. I've given lots of different names over the years, so what does it matter?"

She leaned his way, trying to view him clearly but not conspicuously. "You're totally safe now, Mitch. No one is going to be looking for you anymore. You have my promise."

He lifted an eyebrow. "That's hard for me to believe, Mrs. Gus. You don't know the life I've had to live."

"I think I know enough about you. The party on that night, then the accident."

"It *was* an accident." A glint of a tear showed in his eyes.

"And you've paid a heavy price for what you did. You were going to be a tennis champ. Maybe have a chance to play Wimbledon."

He rocked his chair slightly back and forth. His mind seemed a million miles away. "You have no idea what I lost. What I threw away. No one does. No one ever can."

"That's true. Nobody can. But will you ever stop punishing yourself for Dorothy Hastings?"

The rocking stopped. He faced her fully now. His stubble was developing into a beard. Mostly gray, but with a peppering of brown mixed throughout. Through the damage from additional scars from other fights, she could still see a gentler side of his face. A face that had been young and handsome once. A kind face. A patrician face.

"I don't know how to change this state-of-mind anymore, Mrs. Gus. It's been so long. Prison wasn't the worst of it. I have this continuous dark dialogue with my demons. Year after year of misery. Life becomes a wearying treadmill. I'm so tired of it, exhausted, sick inside, you know? How many nights I've prayed I'd fall asleep and never wake up."

"I know how that feels, Mitch."

He stared without speaking.

"It's true." She looked to the landing outside the open door to see if Father Marcel or Father Jerome were listening. They weren't. "I did something stupid once. A terrible thing. There was…there was a man I hated. With good reason. He was responsible for the death of someone I loved. I've never told this to anybody, Mitch. Please believe me. And I ask you now to never tell what I'm saying. You see, I shot this man because of what he did." She stopped herself, not believing she had spoken those words out loud. After a pause she continued. "And after it was over, I regretted what I did. Despicable though he was, it wasn't for me to take another's life. I loathed myself for it. I wanted to die. Long ago, I used to live in Athens, by the sea. Often I thought about drowning myself. Jumping off some pier at midnight. Slipping away into the cold dark waters."

He listed at full attention while she spoke.

"I just wanted to be forgotten. To rot. Spend eternity in hell, if there really is such a place. In this world, I became both my judge and jury at my trial. I bore witness against myself. I was the prosecutor, and I had no defense. My jury found me guilty. And my sentence was harsh. There was no mercy granted." She shut her eyes and fought to hold back tears, recalling days she struggled so hard to forget. "Year after year I still relive that trial. Even today, although this happened more than two decades ago. So, you see, Alan Mitchell Connery, I'm really not so different than you." She stopped there, finished, sick at heart for dragging this up, and drained to the bone.

After a moment he said, "But you do have a life now. You have your world at the diner. Your friends, your work."

"I do have a life," she agreed. "But I'm still a lost soul, Mitch. Like you. Lost. The mind is its own prison. I know it's too late for me to claim the life you think I have. But one day someone desperate came to me for help. I did everything I could. She had been in danger, badly abused by her husband, but now she was safe. She was so thankful for me. It was then, I think, that I started to realize there were good things I could still do. Not for me, but for others. I could be there if needed to assist other lost souls. Not as some angel, but as a guide, perhaps. Doing for them things I can't do for myself."

"Like the way you've helped me? Father Marcel told me some of the things you've done."

She nodded. "It was the story of how you drifted, always drifting, from place to place, job to job. Mostly, though, drinking yourself unconscious.

Fighting in forsaken bars, even getting arrested again in Seattle. Don't misunderstand me. I don't judge you, Mitch. I want to see you begin to return to your life. If you want to be homeless again, without a bed to call your own, I get it. More punishment. But I was also told you help children at the corner light to cross the street going to school. Why do you do that?"

He made an attempt to smile. His teeth were yellowed from smoke and alcohol. Several were missing from both sides of his wide mouth. He put a hand to the side of his face, looking for an answer. "I guess because somewhere deep down I do like children. They're innocent. They don't know the real world. Yet. Watching them gives me a little moment of peace."

"And is that why you help Ramon with his baseball? That boy adores you, you know? He told me about how you train him, teach him tricks of baseball that could help him become a professional player."

"You know about that?" He genuinely seemed surprised. "I was a baseball fan as a kid, too. I even considered it as a career. I could pitch well. But tennis stole my heart. Compared to that, there was no other competition."

"So, hating yourself as much as you do, you still went to the time and trouble of coaching Ramon. Showing him tricks and tips you'd learned."

"I suppose I did. You're right. Ramon maybe could turn himself into something. Something good. He has the talent. After everything that's happened, I still recognize a gift when I see it."

"Passing on your skill and knowledge to someone is also a gift."

He had no answer to that.

Cora felt that maybe for an instant she had gotten through his thick skin. "And I also know about Javier and his wife. That they cared for you even when you didn't want it."

He sat silent.

"There are good people in the world. Think about it." She pinched the bridge of her nose. Her weariness was showing. "I need to leave in a minute," she said. "Look, I'm not the Salvation Army. But I want to leave you with one thought. If, after you heal, if you decide you like it here, like having your buddy Marcel close, for one. Want to keep teaching Ramon and perhaps other kids, I would be willing to give a helping hand. Way back when, there were those that were there to help me get back on my feet. I'm offering that to you. Want a job in the diner? Earn some money. It's not my business how you spend it. I bet Father Marcel could help you find a room. Ramon would be the happiest kid on the planet. Think about it, Mister Connery. Get better, heal, and think about it. Come by the diner if you decide you like what I'm saying."

She got up, stretched, then went to shake his calloused hand. It was stronger than she anticipated. "Thank you, Mrs. Gus."

"You're welcome, Mitch."

Then she went home to sleep, preparing for a showdown tomorrow. This matter wasn't settled yet.

18

CORA WAS UP BEFORE DAWN. She slept better than she thought she would. A few of the morning staff were surprised to see her so early. She said hi, went into the kitchen and looked over the counter where boxes of fresh produce had been set down.

"Looks surprisingly good today, she muttered to Claude. The head chef had also made it in early this morning. "I'm sorry for coming late this past week. You know what my life has been like..."

Cora waved her hand and stopped him. "Things have been tough for you at home, I know. We'll discuss business later. Let's just be ready to open up."

He nodded and said no more. An assistant, eating a plum from its box, came to help him wash the vegetables and fruit.

It was a gray morning. The weather report spoke of a chance of showers. Rain made the diner less busy at the booths but busier with takeout orders.

Sara Sweeny, at the cash register, standing like a sentry on duty, stood aside as Cora took out the cash box and receipts from yesterday.

One of the first people to enter the diner was Lillian Gorman. She carried an unopened umbrella, a small pocketbook, and glanced around. She was wearing a pair of straight leg slacks, a flowered blue blouse, and a light cardigan on top. When she saw Cora, she greeted her with a loud, "Good morning, Mrs. Gus."

"Sara, keep the money box here. I need to spend a little time with this customer. Unless something urgent comes along try not to disturb us."

"I'll take of everything, Mrs. Gus. Take your time."

Cora beckoned to Lillian Gorman to follow her. Passing the counter, she told the early waiter to bring over two cups of coffee. "This way, Lillian," she said, turning the corner and walking to the farthest table in the back.

They sat. Lillian appeared to be in a good mood. Cora took a chair and gestured for her guest to do the same. In less than a minute the hot coffee was brought with sugar and a small pitcher of half and half.

"Thank you, Paul."

"Just call if you need anything, Mrs. Gus," he said walking away.

"Someone new?" said Lillian, blowing lightly on the steaming coffee.

"He's been here a couple of months. I don't think you know him."

Lillian took her time, setting her umbrella down along the wall behind, picking up the large white porcelain cup and sniffing. "Smells good, as always."

"Enjoy."

Neither woman spoke for a couple of minutes. Both sipped coffee and casually watched new diners taking a booth. Three businessmen. Familiar people that worked in the insurance offices down the block. The owner of the local pet store, Aldo Margolis, was sitting on the end seat at the counter, eating a plate of scrambled eggs and toast.

At length, Lillian said, "I appreciate your phone call last night, Mrs. Gus. I hope the news you want to share is good."

Cora took a few long moments before answering. "I expected it to be better, I'm sorry to say."

Lillian's eyebrows rose. She put one hand to her hair, feeling good about her recent haircut and coloring. "Oh?"

"I don't know how to say this, but…" She drew a long deep breath. "I expected to find our homeless man on the mend. Unfortunately, that's not what happened."

"Not what happened? What did happen? I'm not following you."

"Well, Lillian. I did a lot of checking things out, as you had asked. It was hard at first, but I found out a few interesting facts from the hospital. They discharged him, you know, and he found somewhere he could hide while recovering."

Lillian drank more coffee.

"Would you like a refill? On the house."

"Yes, please."

Cora signaled to the busboy, but the waiter also saw her and came hurrying over. "There you go, ladies," he said, filling both cups to the brim. And off he went, happy to please the boss and her friend.

"You were saying, Mrs. Gus?"

"I'll give it to you straight, Lillian. No bullshit. As I mentioned last night, your homeless friend had been seen recently hanging out in the evenings in the park behind St. Joseph's church."

"Certainly. It's close by, and I've been going there myself for some years. I'm not Catholic, but I have to say that the priests there really take care of things. It's a lovely little park. We're so fortunate to have it."

"True. They have a gardener, and I'm told some local people, probably parishioners, help out too. Lovely trees and bushes. Flowers are in bloom there now."

Cora could see that Lillian was becoming a bit frustrated, eager to hear the news. "Anyway, Lillian. I was sure Matt, your homeless man, would show up. You know, to relax. Maybe get some sun. His body needs lots of healing."

"I'm sure it does. But you didn't see him, Mrs. Gus?"

With lowered eyes, Cora said, "I did see him. He was on the ground, unmoving. Three squad cars were there, lights flashing, stopping passersby from entering the park."

"What are you saying?"

"Last evening. Someone…Someone took a knife to this poor guy. Stabbed him repeatedly. It was a horrible sight. Blood all over the body. He was dead. There was nothing to be done."

Lillian put a hand to her mouth. "No. It's not possible. It can't be." She closed her eyes as if saying a brief prayer. "You said he was found alive…"

"That was before. I was so eager to call you and tell you good news. It never occurred to me that anything like this might happen. I feel so bad. I mislead you. I didn't mean to." She looked at the older woman as she picked up her own coffee cup and drank.

"Then he is dead." Lillian became quiet.

"Now it's a matter of finding his killer."

"Are there any clues? You have all these friends among the police. I wish I had your contacts. It there any idea of who was responsible? I mean, someone has to be caught. They can't just get away with a thing like this. Killing a poor homeless man."

Cora sat patiently listening to Lillian complain about rising crime, how dangerous it was now for people, particularly the elderly and infirm, to walk the streets at night. How something needed to be done. Useless politicians, lazy cops, uncaring citizens. How different it all was when she was young. How safe the streets were, how the city mayors took personal tours of the neighborhoods.

"You're right, Lillian. But you know, one thing catches my attention. This homeless man you said you were so concerned about. You haven't even asked me if I found out his name."

Lillian backed up slightly. Her eyes narrowed. "I don't understand. His name? You told me. It was Matt. That's what he called himself to me, remember?"

"Oh, I do remember. Better than you realize. Cora reached inside the pocket of the apron she was wearing and took out a folded piece of paper, which she carefully unfolded on the flat surface of the table. She kept her forefinger on the paper. "I have the name here. The full, proper name,"

Lillian Gorman sighed. She looked at the folded paper and sighed again. "I guess it isn't so important anymore, is it? If he died, I suppose it doesn't matter."

"You don't seem very upset."

"Well," she stalled for words. "Of course, I'm upset. Who wouldn't be? A decent fellow down on his luck. First, he's beaten half to death, then killed. My lord, what terrible times we live in. Such a shame. Such a pity."

"I'll tell you his name anyway. You deserve to know it. You were so worried when you came to me, asked for my help. Practically begged me to get involved."

"Well, I didn't know who else to turn to, Mrs. Gus. Everyone knows you know how to get things done. And I'm grateful. But now that he's gone..."

"You'll be interested in the name."

"I will?"

Cora picked up the paper, looking over the top at Lillian Gorman. "His real identity was Alan...Alan Mitchell Connery."

Lillian's hand trembled as she put her cup back into the saucer. "I think I need to be going now. I have to get to the post office. You know how crowded they get when you arrive late." She folded with her napkin and made ready to leave.

"Don't go yet. I have more news to tell you."

"More news?" she seemed confused and perturbed.

"Make yourself comfortable, Lillian. I think you'll want to hear the rest also." Her tone was more of a demand than a request.

"I don't understand what this is about, Mrs. Gus. I'm grateful for your time, but what else is there to say?"

"Plenty." Cora kept a fixed gaze on Lillian. It made her guest feel uncomfortable. "I have an admission to make. You see, I haven't been totally honest with you this morning." She made a face. "I guess you could say I lied."

"You lied? I'm totally mystified. What's going on, Mrs. Gus? What did you lie about?"

"Alan. Alan Connery. You see, he isn't dead. Actually, he's very much alive. And he is healing. Better than you might expect, considering."

"What are you saying? Why are you telling me this? Are you trying to make a fool out of me?"

"No, Lillian. Quite the opposite. It's *you* who was trying to make a fool out of *me*."

"This is insane, Mrs. Gus. Stop this nonsense. I have to leave."

"Stay in your chair." She took out her phone. "I have a photo I'd like to show you."

Lillian shook her head. "I don't want to see any of you damn photos. Leave me alone."

"Not just yet. Look." She slid the phone to the other side of the table. Lillian stared down at the picture. She gasped. It was a photo of a man holding a large knife at his side. The photo was a profile, and even though he was wearing a hoodie she could make out some features. A few stood out. Broad nose, jutting chin.

"Any idea who this man is?" said Cora in a cold voice.

"No. I don't."

"Look again. Here, I'll enlarge the face so you can see it better."

In a loud voice, Lillian said, "No. I don't want to see it."

The owner of the Athena Diner made it bigger anyway, and then held it up. Lillian turned her head away. "Take a good hard look, Lillian Gorman. That is your married name, right? Lillian Gorman. Your husband was Rudy."

"Rudy was a good, hard-working man. I loved him. A pillar of the community. He passed away a few years back, leaving me a widow. You know that. You were at his funeral. And you sent flowers and donated to a charity in his name. What are you trying to do? I want to go."

"You'll be out of here in a few minutes. You have my word."

"This conversation, or whatever we're having is extremely bad for my nerves. I don't know what you think you are doing, but I don't like it—and I won't stand for it."

"You'll stay until I'm done." Cora raised her voice and a few people noticed. "Know the guy in the photo you just looked at?" Lillian refused to answer. "His name is Kyle. A gullible man if you ask me. Kyle Hastings is his full name. He flew here from California not long ago. That knife he's carrying. That's the knife intended for Alan Connery. Your homeless friend. The one you wanted me to find for you."

"I have no idea what the hell you're talking about."

"You asked me to do some research, didn't you? Well, I did. I also was able to get more info from the DMV. The Department of Motor Vehicles."

Lillian began to twist uncomfortably. She squeezed a tissue in her hand again and again.

"Feeling warm, Lillian? The air not cool enough? I can have them turn it down. Although I don't think that's what's bothering you." She looked to the busboy. "Bring us some water with ice, please."

"Whatever you must be thinking Mrs. Gus, is wrong."

The ice water was delivered. Lillian took a few large swallows. Cora waited patiently until she was done.

"Let's see. She looked at her paper again, drumming her fingers. "You and Rudy were married here in New York, I see. More than twenty-five years ago. I bet it was a nice wedding. Was your family there?"

"Rudy's parents and brothers. Some of my family. I'm getting tired of your constant questions. This isn't some court. I'm not on trial."

"Aren't you? I think you are. You were the only person who knew about the homeless man going to the park in the evening."

At that Lillian sat chilled. A malevolent look came into her eyes.

"I see that after your wedding you settled down in New York, in Queens County, and soon you applied for your New York driver's license. I have a photocopy in my bag. Want to see it?"

She made no response.

"And interestingly I made a note. Naturally, you turned in your California license. It had a different surname back then. Your maiden name. It says here, you were born in Ventura, California." She met the cold stare with one of her own. "Maiden name, how curious, Lillian Hastings."

Silence ensued. Lillian stopped fidgeting. She put her arms on the table, no longer with shaky hands. "What do you think you're trying to prove?"

"Prove? Take out your cell phone. I think you were expecting a call from your nephew Kyle Hastings that never came. Maybe a text last night? But there wasn't one. You know why he didn't call last night? Because he took the midnight Delta redeye home to Los Angeles. By now he's landed, probably driving back to Westwood, where he lives with his family. But you know all that. Don't believe me? Go on, Lillian, try giving a call."

Lillian Gorman was jolted. Blood drained from her face, she felt as though she'd been kicked in the stomach. She shuddered at the relentless flow of accusations, listening with amazement at the abundance of information this amateur investigator gathered in recent days. Yet, if she had underestimated Mrs. Gus, her tormentor would promptly realize that she'd been underestimated as well.

"If you think I'll crack under pressure, I won't," she said with a cool taunt. "This is all circumstantial claptrap. You may have good informants, but that won't get you anywhere. You expect you'll snag me somehow, but you won't."

"I don't have to snag you. You did that yourself. You see, I know all about you, dear Lillian. Dorothy Hastings was your sister. Your flesh and blood. And you've clung tightly onto this hatred all your life. Seething with never ending bitterness for the man who hit her and took her life. Reviled him, swore payback no matter how long it took."

At that, Lillian snickered sourly. "Calling it 'hate' doesn't go far enough. I despise him like human compost. Lowest of the lowest trash. Pig swill. I prayed for years he would die in prison. Raped, beaten, having his throat slit. To die lonely and petrified. And seeing the face of my poor sister, laughing while he slithers down to hell."

"So, you spent years poisoning Kyle's mind with your vitriol. From his childhood. Over time, you taught him to hate as much as you. He likely would have grown into a healthy, mature adult if you hadn't badgered and harassed him most of his life. Making him relive that night over and over, so that he mirrored your enmity."

"What do you know about it? My sister Dorothy was a nurse. She *saved* lives, not took them. A loving woman, a good mother, who comforted her patients, and was loyal to her husband and family." She spat into the empty cup. "Well-bred Alan Connery, drunk and high in his fancy car, running late, rushing to sign tennis contracts. Four years behind bars, he served. Four miserable years. Then he walked free. That parasite. I visited my sister's grave a hundred times. I swore he would eventually pay..." Both her hands clenched into fists.

"Vengeance is sweet, huh Lillian?" said Cora, incensed. "Retaliation at last. You thought over the implications of killing Alan yourself, if you had the nerve. But you don't. That would dirty your hands. You orchestrated all of it. You put it all onto Kyle. Twisted his head. You didn't give a damn if you turned that innocent boy into a killer. You didn't even care if Kyle got caught. Only that Alan Connery would be dead. That was all that mattered."

Spittle flew from her lips. "How dare you! You're a holier than thou egotistical nothing."

"And you're a hideous woman, Lillian Gorman. Somehow you located where Alan Connery was, one way or another you tracked him down. First in Seattle. Having Kyle hunt him down where lowlife drunks go for cheap booze, and then purposely pick a quarrel with him in a mean streets bar. Alan already had a criminal record, so naturally he was the one to get blamed, finding himself thrown back in jail."

Lillian bristled. "What gall you have, taking the side of a murderer! Year after year I kept begging heaven I'd locate this seedy tramp. This drunken, worthless piece of shit." She scowled, face contorted, feeling she was an avenging angel swooping down. "When I told you about the homeless man helping me with shopping bags, that was the truth. All this time him sitting on a box on our streets. What a cruel joke. After all these years I didn't recognize him. Who would?" She gloated at her next thought. "But on one of those days, when he carried my heavy bags for a dollar tip, I recognized something familiar about his voice. He said some words how I remembered him speaking at trial. I'd attended that courtroom every single day. I studied him carefully, this wretched miscreant pleading for mercy. That day when I realized his identity I nearly choked. The posture, those shuffling steps, they belonged to the same man. I looked deeply into those eyes. Those light blue despondent eyes. People's features change, faces wrinkle, but eyes, the eyes stay the same. I realized I was looking once more at the murderer of my sister. Here he was in New York. Coming to me. The same felon, right here. An alcoholic, self-pitying failure. My heart pounded in my chest. Yes, I phoned my nephew. I was in a tizzy to tell him I'd found the killer of his mother. After all these long years. At last. I could almost feel Kyle's own revulsion rise through the phone. Yes, I planned it, damn right."

"You made one big mistake, Lillian," Cora said calmly. "You thought you could use *me*. Arrange me as a part of your scheme after Kyle botched it the first time. Alan was yelling too loud. Someone heard and saw from the window. A witness. You told me that yourself. The job only half done, Kyle ran away like a coward, leaving a helpless human being laying soaked in blood and rain near the gutter."

"I didn't use you, Mrs. Gus." Lillian protested. "I sought your help. I asked you to try and locate him. I knew your reputation as a would-be detective. Knew you'd bite. I only needed to find his location. I'd take care of the rest. Oh yes."

Cora stood to her full height and stared hard at the bitter old woman opposite. "You're a hateful bitch."

"You think I don't know a few things about you, Mrs. Gus? I've been coming to this diner for a long, long time. And I remember Gus very well. I even recall back when he brought you to work here. Your first job in America. You acted like this aristocratic, poor innocent creature shipped from Greece. Hanging onto Gus like a leech. Making poor old Gus fall for you. Oh, I heard stories. More than a few. Some trouble back home, wasn't there? Talk said your family had to get you out. Find you a new home. You think you're better than me. Well, you're not. You're a low-class loser like so many foreigners. Gus was blinded by you. What a fool."

Their voices were growing louder, and both diners and staff stared. The entire diner became quiet.

Cora stood her ground, unperturbed by the tirade. She lowered her voice. "In this crazy world we're all actors in a sordid story, Lillian. After all your invective you could still be charged as an accessory to attempted murder."

"Accessory? For what?"

"For the first attack on Alan Connery. And also charged with aiding and abetting your nephew this second time. Did that nice shiny knife Kyle was carrying come from your kitchen?"

At that Lillian recoiled.

"Right now, I'm giving Kyle the break you never gave him. The chance to go home and live a good, fulfilling life with his family. Far, far away from you. The police say Alan Connery's made no legal complaint—yet. By the way, I have the shiny kitchen knife Kyle was holding in the photo. Keep it a very safe place. Your nephew's fingerprints are all over it. Maybe a few of yours, too? My insurance policy against any new assault. Keep that in mind. If you or anyone else tries to harm Connery again, I'll be coming straight for you. I won't have to search you out. And this time it *will* be personal."

Lillian Gorman avoided eye contact. She recognized Mrs. Gus was not someone you chose to turn into an enemy. Trying to maintain her bearing and dignity, she collected her bag and her umbrella. Before she had a chance to walk away, Cora said, "Don't ever show your face in the Athena again. Leave now, quietly, while I let you. And you know I mean it."

Cora watched while the older woman turned to leave.

"Hey Lillian." she said.

Lillian turned back around to face Cora's smoldering eyes.

"Don't forget to look both ways each time you cross the street."

Closing came a little early that night. Cora assisted with the daily chores, including setting the tables and mopping the floors for the next morning's opening. She walked alone down the empty street after the diner's lights were shut and the door was locked. Eddie Coltrane offered her a lift. She declined, even though it was still drizzling. Her thoughts returned to Athens, to the life she had enjoyed and lost, and then back to the present, with the new life she had created. She no longer believed there was a chance to regain her own world of happiness. However, she was certain she could be there for other lost souls. If they were in trouble, or in crisis and didn't have anywhere else to turn.

That was Cora's true calling. Assisting those down on their luck, overwhelmed when life kicks you in the face. Desperate for a helping hand, seeking to obtain justice in an unfair world. This was her role, likely until her final days on this earth. Perhaps someday this may help in quelling her own darkness. And with this came a renewed sense of identity.

She remembered she needed to phone Hunter, aware how eager he would be to hear the full story of her confrontation with Lillian Gorman. And maybe afterward she could reciprocate.

Her gaze drifted up to the dreary sky. She whispered, Gus you saved my life, and gave me a new one. Dirk, you still have my heart. You taught me more than you'll ever know. Rest in peace wherever you are.

She pulled down her cap, put her hands into her raincoat pockets, and made her way home.

COMING SOON!

The next mystery thriller of

MRS GUS and the

DINER OF LOST SOULS